Shotgun Lullabies

Conversation Pieces

A Small Paperback Series from Aqueduct Press

1. The Grand Conversation
   Essays by L. Timmel Duchamp

2. With Her Body
   Short Fiction by Nicola Griffith

3. Changeling
   A Novella by Nancy Jane Moore

4. Counting on Wildflowers
   An Entanglement by Kim Antieau

5. The Traveling Tide
   Short Fiction by Rosaleen Love

6. The Adventures of the Faithful Counselor
   A Narrative Poem by Anne Sheldon

7. Ordinary People
   A Collection by Eleanor Arnason

8. Writing the Other: A Practical Approach
   by Nisi Shawl & Cynthia Ward

9. Alien Bootlegger
   A Novella by Rebecca Ore

10. The Red Rose Rages (Bleeding)
    A Short Novel by L. Timmel Duchamp

11. Talking Back
    Epistolary Fantasies
    edited by L. Timmel Duchamp

12. Absolute Uncertainty
    Short Fiction by Lucy Sussex

13. Candle in a Bottle
    A Novella by Carolyn Ives Gilman

14. Knots
    Short Fiction by Wendy Walker

15. Naomi Mitchison: A Profile of Her Life and Work
    A Monograph by Lesley A. Hall

16. We, Robots
    A Novella by Sue Lange

17. Making Love in Madrid
    A Novella by Kimberly Todd Wade

18. Of Love and Other Monsters
    A Novella by Vandana Singh

19. Aliens of the Heart
    Short Fiction by Carolyn Ives Gilman

20. Voices From Fairyland:
    The Fantastical Poems of Mary Coleridge, Charlotte
    Mew, and Sylvia Townsend Warner
    Edited and With Poems by Theodora Goss

21. My Death
    A Novella by Lisa Tuttle

22. De Secretis Mulierum
    A Novella by L. Timmel Duchamp

23. Distances
    A Novella by Vandana Singh

24. Three Observations and a Dialogue:
    Round and About SF
    Essays by Sylvia Kelso and a correspondence
    with Lois McMaster Bujold

25. The Buonarotti Quartet
    Short Fiction by Gwyneth Jones

26. Slightly Behind and to the Left
    Four Stories & Three Drabbles
    by Claire Light

27. Through the Drowsy Dark
    Short Fiction and Poetry
    by Rachel Swirsky

28. Shotgun Lullabies
    Stories and Poems by Sheree Renée Thomas

29. A Brood of Foxes
    A Novella by Kristin Livdahl

About the Aqueduct Press Conversation Pieces Series

The feminist engaged with sf is passionately interested in challenging the way things are, passionately determined to understand how everything works. It is my constant sense of our feminist-sf present as a grand conversation that enables me to trace its existence into the past and from there see its trajectory extending into our future. A genealogy for feminist sf would not constitute a chart depicting direct lineages but would offer us an ever-shifting, fluid mosaic, the individual tiles of which we will probably only ever partially access. What could be more in the spirit of feminist sf than to conceptualize a genealogy that explicitly manifests our own communities across not only space but also time?

Aqueduct's small paperback series, Conversation Pieces, aims to both document and facilitate the "grand conversation." The Conversation Pieces series presents a wide variety of texts, including short fiction (which may not always be sf and may not necessarily even be feminist), essays, speeches, manifestoes, poetry, interviews, correspondence, and group discussions. Many of the texts are reprinted material, but some are new. The grand conversation reaches at least as far back as Mary Shelley and extends, in our speculations and visions, into the continually-created future. In Jonathan Goldberg's words, "To look forward to the history that will be, one must look at and retell the history that has been told." And that is what Conversation Pieces is all about.

L. Timmel Duchamp

Jonathan Goldberg, "The History That Will Be" in Louise Fradenburg and Carla Freccero, eds., *Premodern Sexualities* (New York and London: Routledge, 1996)

Published by Aqueduct Press
PO Box 95787
Seattle, WA 98145-2787
www.aqueductpress.com

Cover illustration: *Shotguns* by John Biggers (1924-2001), 1987, oil
and acrylic painting on canvas, 42" x 49 7/8" inches.
Courtesy of Eugene Foney, Artcetera, Houston, TX.

http://www.maineantiquedigest.com/stories/?id=1698

Book Design by Kathryn Wilham
Original Block Print of Mary Shelley by Justin Kempton:
www.writersmugs.com

Printed in the USA by Applied Digital Imaging

Conversation Pieces
Volume 28

Shotgun Lullabies

Stories and Poems
by
Sheree Renée Thomas

Grateful Acknowledgment to the Editors and Publishers of the following works:

"Invocation" appeared as "Lore" in *Southern Revival: Deep Magic for Hurricane Katrina* edited by Tamara Kaye Sellman (2006).

"How Sukie Cross de Big Wata" first appeared in *Mojo: Conjure Stories* edited by Nalo Hopkinson (Warner Books, 2004).

"Once" and "Untitled Scratch Poem, featuring River" appeared in *Mythic Delirium 2* edited by Mike Allen (Mythic Delirium Books, 2006) and in *The 2006 Rhysling Awards: Year's Best Science Fiction Poetry* (Science Fiction Poetry Association, 2007).

"Bender's Bow" and "Touch" appeared in *Colorlines: The national magazine of race and politics* edited by Daisy Hernandez (Nov/Dec 2006 and Mar/Apr 2008).

"Visitation of the Oracle at McKain Street" appeared in another form as "Survivor at rest" in *Hurricane Blues: Poems about Katrina and Rita* edited by Philip C. Kolin and Susan Swartwout (Southeast Missouri State University Press, 2006).

"Malaika Descending" appeared in *Bronx Biannual 2: The Literary Journal of Urbane Urban Literature* edited by Miles Marshall Lewis (Akashic Press, 2007).

"Djarkarta Rising" appeared in *2001: A Science Fiction Poetry Anthology* (Anamnesis Press, 2002) and in *The 2002 Rhysling Awards: Year's Best Speculative Poetry* (Speculative Fiction Poetry Association, 2003).

"Sky in West Memphis" appeared in *The Ringing Ear: Black Southern Poetry* edited by Nikky Finney (University of Georgia Press, 2007) and in *Cave Canem IX*.

Table of Contents

Sukie Diamond...

Invocation	4
How Sukie Cross De Big Wata	5
How Sukie Come Free	6
How Sukie Left Sippi	10

...Shotgun lullabies

Once	18
Untitled Old Scratch Poem, featuring River	20
Bender's Bow	22
Visitation of the Oracle at McKain Street	41
Bottom Rock	44
Lodestone, or laying the trick	46
Malaika Descending	48
Dust	63
Touch	64
Sky in West Memphis	81

Djarkarta rising...

epiphany at Djarkarta	84
Jigganaut	85
Djarkarta rising	87
The Grassdreaming Tree	89

Sukie Diamond…

Invocation

In the beginning God walked barefoot 'cross the land. She spread Her big toe wide 'cross the rich, deep earth and danced. She stomped so hard with Her rock-bottom feet, the earth split right open. Still She danced. Her big toe sunk deep, and the sweet waters rise quick, quick. That's how we got the rivers, and the lakes, and the creeks.

Still God danced.

She shook Her wide hips and dipped so low, the air blow. That's how we got wind, from God's sweet hip sway. She danced. Cross brown dirt and red clay, Her toes digging valleys in the moist earth, heels rocking, flat plains unfolding, rolling under the balls of Her ashy feet. Still God danced. Mountains forming under the high high arch of her stepping feet. Danced, the earth yielding under the weight of her pretty toes. Danced so hard She sweat, salt rolling in big drops down Her chin and her nose. Danced 'til she cried, salt rolling into the waters 'til we got the oceans and the seas.

Still God Danced. Hot-footed 'cross burning sands in the desert, shaking her hips, *bump bump diddy rump* 'til the earth quake and the trees sprout from seeds. Still God Danced, 'til her wide black toes touched every part of the land, soles slapped against every speck of dirt and sand. God danced 'til her feet were tired, so sore she had to sit, rest her tailbone down on a high bluff, wipe the sweat from her eye and spit, dip her feet in a cool sip of water, river-deep. The black earth so thick, a rich crust caking the bottom of Her feet, 'til the river turn to mud, and we got the Mississippi.

～ ～

How Sukie Cross de Big Wata

Before you begin, before you fix your lips to tell the lie, let me see if I can take this tale and bend it straight. I was there when her bloodline first arrived, when her mama folk emerged from tree-borne ships, 'cause I carried them on my back, carried them from the door of no return in the land they call Mother, and I been carrying them ever since. Sayna, 'cause the wood is a witness, and I ain't talking bout no slippery elm or no weeping, whimpering willow tree. Sayna, I'm talking 'bout baobab, mahogany, banyon, mapou, and ebon tree-borne ships that carried those that did not fly away, carried those that did not jump 'cross bloody bows and plunge deep into my depths. Ain't talking bout those who walked back 'cross my neck to their father's shores but those who come 'cross the waters on spiritwood, on my turtleback and limbs outstretched to the land they call Taino, the land in the backdoor of what they call New World.

These lives I carried, while the hollerwood splintered and echoed, their groans creaking like split-bone in the wood. I carried them, her people 'cross the big

5

watas, and I carried her like I carried the rest—generations 'cross the crying watas to these bitter shores.

So when she dipped her long black toe in my throat, the part they call Sippi—*and the child did not speak*—I asked her did she know my name. *Child*, I say, the muddy waters carrying my words to the riverbank where she stood, *do you know me?* She blink at me like she ain't sure she heard right, so I send a cold current swirling round her toes. *Child*, I say, and I say it again. *Do know your own name? Do you know your mama name?* At the mention of her mama, this womanchile look like she want to sink, not swim, so I send a warm current to tickle the black bottom of her feet. How you gon' 'cross over these watas so wide and dip into that other world, if you don't even know yourself? If you can guess my name, I will tell you a story. And if you listen true, you will know when I am bending it and when I am telling it straight, 'cause like a river, every story got a bend. So, listen, child, and I will carry you, carry you clear over, like I carry all the rest. Carry you from where you come, to where you must go.

~ ~

How Sukie Come Free

She has many names. Aunt Nancy, Sukie Diamond, Diamond Free, but her navel name was Stella or Dinah, depending on who tell the tale. I'm telling this, and on my end of the river bottom, we called her Stella because no matter who come after her, she always managed to steal away. Now, some folk say Stella mama was a real bad seed, contrary kind of soul, always running. Say the last time she run, her whitefolks dug a hole in the ground and put her in there, belly baby-swole and all, and beat her 'til she couldn't do nothing but grunt. Say when she come out of that hole that night, she was spirit-talking, whispering words ain't no body live long enough to know the meaning to. Saying,

Stee la dee nah
nah dee la stee
stee la dee nah
nah dee la stee
steeeela! deenah!
Steela! Steela!

Whispering then shouting and yelling them words, part African, part Indian, 'til folk turn a pot over to hold in the song, whispering and shouting 'til she didn't speak no more and her body come still. But her baby, that baby Stella just a kicking in the belly. Folk say they could see her little arms and legs just a waving under the cold dead flesh of her mama. Say Stella birth herself in her owntime, say she come on out kicking and swinging, too, and been swinging ever since.

Say when she was born, her eyes was wide open, not shuteye like most babies but bright as two harvest moons. Say she leaned back, took in her world, saw her mama tree-stump dead—the spirit still fresh on her breath—and didn't drop no tears. No, Stella didn't cry. Stella leaned back, smacked the old granny that held her, and snatched back her navel string. Say she'd bury it her own damned self. Say she'd rather carry her destiny in her own hands than trust it to some strange bloodtree, cut down 'fore its roots can grow like her mama and all her kin that come before. And some folk say she been carrying that string in a mojo band 'round her waist ever since.

But that night, the night Stella birthed herself, they say she looked round and saw the others' faces and said just as loud for anybody to hear, "I'll eat the clay of my own grave 'fore I'll slave a day in this life or the next, for any man, woman, child or spirit—white, negra, or other." She say this, and then she was gone.

Stella walked right down the path to massa's house, spit, and set the Big House afire. Then the fields; then the tool shack that held every hoe. She kept walking 'til she come 'cross overseer, crook-legged and buck-toe, running from all them burning fields.

Now, overseer was looking mighty 'fraid 'til he see Stella standing up in the row, buck-naked with the backside of a smile on her face. When he saw Stella frowning down at him, he dug his rusty heels into the ground and puff up his chest 'til his black muscles gleamed 'neath all the sweat and dust.

"Where you think you headed, gal?" he asked, like the aim of Stella's long toes wasn't cuss clear. "Who yo' people?"

Now, overseer didn't recognize Stella, but he look her up and down like he thirsty and want a taste. At first sight, Stella didn't say nothing, but her eyes walked all over his face. Seem like she knowed he was the one put her mama in the bellyhole and beat her 'til she spoke in spirit tongue. (What overseer didn't know was that Stella remembered what most forget, on the trip to this world from the next. She knew why she'd been sent, just not how or when or where. She reckoned she'd just put one foot 'fore the next 'til they carried her to a place that felt like home. But when she come out that night, she knew that bellyhole wasn't it.)

Finally, after a long, hard spell, Stella say, "My mama folk come from heavy-boned ships…" She spit, and sparks fly. "They'se the kind the slavers couldn't half handle…" She spit and mo sparks fly. "…and if you couldn't handle my mama…" Spit, she moving now, "…what make you think you can handle me?"

When she says this, overseer look like he grab the wrong end of a rattler. "Who yo' mama, girl?" he ask, backing up all a sudden.

"Bet you know when I give you this kiss," Stella say, pressing her full lips on his rusty jaw—and burnt off half his face. Overseer cry so loud, his voice seem to come from a hundred throats, distant but close-like.

"*Steela! Steela!*" he cry. She watched him in silence and frowned. Seem like her name in his mouth called down the rain. Stella stood under the baptism a moment, the sky a red sinking ball afire, then she picked up her long feet to go.

When overseer come tumbling down the row, jaw looking like a big ole greasy piece of fatback, folk was ripping and running so, nobody had time to see Stella make her way down the road, through the gates, and on into them woods. And that's how Sukie come free. She walked her way into freedom, carrying that navel string in her hand.

The nail ain't broke
the nail just bent
and that's the way
the story went

⌣ ⌣

How Sukie Left Sippi

After Sukie walked down to massa's house, spit, and set the Big House afire, then the fields, the tool shack that held every hoe, and the overseer down in cotton row, folk was ripping and running so, nobody had time to see her make her way down the road, through the gates, and on into the woods. Some folk say that's how she come free, walking her way into freedom, carrying her navel string in her hand.

But that night, the sky was full of cloud-splitters, and the rain felt like heavy hands pounding the earth. In the woods, the tree branches made dark arches, and Sukie ducked beneath them 'til her feet carried her 'cross upturned roots and thorny thickets to an elder-spirit tree whose branches curved just so.

Back then, the woods stayed full of negras, spirits, and haints. Folk running all the time, even if it only for a few days or a week or two, 'til they hear the Word—that being that massa wouldn't turn a lick if they come back within a day of his calling. In them time, a negra could come back when massa say or get the nine and thirty—lashes, that is. Come back or run away for good.

Now, Sukie didn't run. She *walked*. She walked right on through the plum thickets and bilderbrush weeds, and climbed up in that elder tree. Guess she knew then not a bull had been born or a lash made evil enough to break the hard skin on her cold blackflesh. She chuckled to herself 'cause poor overseer never got a chance to give her back a taste. Still, Sukie shut her eyes for a spell and dreamed 'til she woke to see a Screech Owl sitting on her branch. Owl was just a-fidgeting and whispering, shaking his great head. Owl say,

Oooh wee Sukie
oooh wee Sukie
sho'll in trouble now
oooh wee Sukie
oooh wee Sukie
massa done sent bloodhounds
better get gone
'fore trouble get grown
your scent all over de ground
if they find you
you know what they gone do
nine and thirty lashes
oooh wee oooh!

Now, Sukie stretch and yawn, blink back remnants of the day. Look old Screech Owl dead in his face and spit. The branch spark and sizzle a l'il in the drizzling dusk. Sukie say, she ain't worried bout no lash 'cause ain't n'am person gon' lay a finger or a scar on her back or leg. Say she heal 'fore the blood rise warm. And can't no man, slaver, teacher, or preacher claim the backroom of her body, mind, or soul. Say she walk in the guts and scales of holy rollers and got a mojo bone buried deep in her breast. Say she come here, head so full of figurin' and words so old and new, the books still waiting on the seeds to take root—let alone the trees. Say she don't need no pass nor no word from massa. Sukie say she go where she very well please. She say massa got more than her flat feet on his mind. Say massa still be stomping out that big ole fire she start, long after she come and gone. Sukie say this and smile, like she know a secret, and Screech Owl hoot, too. He knowed can't nobody get a hold of Sukie 'cause she a dangerous kind of hussy, a negra gal, damn near one of the most dangerous of all.

Screech Owl knowed this but still he worry. He knowed Sukie whatn't nothing but a day old, and a young'un sitting in newborn skin—no matter how thick and spirit-blessed—still needed a mother's wing in the world.

True, though Sukie had birthed herself in her own-time, climbing from her mama's bone-still womb, and she'd come out kicking and swinging, too. Not shuteye like most natural born babies, but eyes wide open like two harvest moons, *boop!* Sitting up in the sky. Sukie had spoken her first words with a mouth full of teeth and not a tear in her eye, breaking the stunned silence of the others who'd watched her walk away to her doom—or so they thought. And she'd spoken in spirit-tongue, as her mama before her death, rising from the bellyhole to take her freedom, her long feet leading her straight to Screech Owl's elderspirit tree.

Now, Sukie done all that in a woman's fullgrown body that ain't yet seen one day of sun, let alone two, but inside, her heart was grieving. Seem like the l'il sleep she got was nothing but a drop of sorrow, the taste as bittersweet as wada root and all them big words in her mouth. And for the first time since Sukie climb out her mama womb, seem like she could barely breathe. Her chest felt tight, the breasts heavy with mama-ache and the phantom weight of stolen freedom. She knew there wasn't but one place she could go to relieve it.

'fore Screech Owl could blink and turn his big wobbly head, Sukie was up stretching her long limbs, shaking the elder bark out of her ears, brushing the grief from her eyes and her thick, tangled hair. She was headed for the bellyhole, where they'd buried her mama.

"Owl, I thanks you for the company," Sukie say, "but I'ma have to see 'bout my way."

Sukie leapt from the elderspirit's dark, knotty branches and landed on moist fertile ground. Turned her straight back to go.

Screech Owl could tell by the curve of her hip sway that Sukie wasn't going to turn back. Still he hopped down to a lower branch, his big ole eyes blinking in the dark, crying,

Aaah Sukie, Aaah Sukie
know it's yo' mama you mourn
but you better turn west
where your fortune be best
or them pattyrollers
gon' make you wish
you whatn't born!

Now, Sukie turn her back on Screech Owl, didn't want to hear another mumbling word, but seem like somebody call her name, and it whatn't no owl either. The call echoed from the pit of her own belly, sound like sweet spirits singin'. Then Sukie felt a kiss, soft full lips on her temple, the place where the spirit rest, and she knew it was her mama come to visit.

Sukie shut her eyes, head bowed as blue flames licked her brown skin and slowly spread round the curve of her jaw to her throat. She felt strong arms round her, a bosom that pulsed not with blood but with will, and shoulders as wide as her own.

Sukie stood there, among the elder trees in the south bank of massa's land, embracing the body that for a time had sheltered her own from a world that would make her unfree. Sukie stood there, cradling her mama's head in her arms, breathing—*one mississippi, two mississippi, three mississippi, breathe.* Then her mama spirit disappeared, and Sukie was alone again. She turned her face toward the earth, listening with strained ears for the sound of many movements, sounds dragged off like heavy bails of cotton.

Overhead, the sky opened up, as if to welcome her mama spirit, washing the bloodstains of each moment she'd breathed from the soil. Sukie rose from her square knees and drank skywater, fat drops glistening on her chin.

Soon, she knew, she must leave that place. The Sippi couldn't hold her body no more than it could her mama spirit. The air around her grew dense, thick with spirits, the ancestors pressing against her skin, pushing her forward. Sukie moved as if invisible fingers were gently coaxing her to go. She moved with heavy feet, allowing the black dirt so full of cottonseed, blood, and bone to fall heavily to the earth through stiff fingers.

Sukie moved with purpose, flinging more of the black mud with each step, until all that remained of her mama's charred body were a few dark smudges on her fingertips and lips.

~

Some folk say when Sukie got to the river, she turned herself into a stone. You know the kind, smooth and polished and slick. The kind of rock that'll slip out of your fingers if you ain't careful, bust you in your own head. Well, one of them pattyrollers, surprised not to find Sukie barefoot and bleeding on the water's edge, seized a stone just like that one and chunked it clear 'cross the water, clear to the other side of the river, saying that's how he'd bust that negra gal's head if he ever caught sight of her again.

Now, when the stone reached the other side and settled in the dust, it turned into Sukie's straight back again, and Sukie just wiped the dust off her long feet and smile and pointed her long toes west, sangin'—

> Steela Deenah Steela
> Steela Deenah Steela
> sho'll glad to put Sippi to rest
> guess these feets is heading west
> there's a wagon train calling my name
> leaving Sippi, won't be back again
> call me Sukie Diamond
> changed to a stone
> skipped 'cross the river

and now I'm gone
diamond to a stone a stone turned to gold
on my way to the Oregon road

And that's how Sukie left Sippi. She skipped her way clear 'cross the river.

The nail ain't broke
the nail just bent
and that's the way
the story went

…Shotgun lullabies

Once

we said thunder
   was Old Sista Sky
            picking out her naps
      untangling the knots
in her kitchen
lightning was Old Sista
           firing up her hot comb
      the mist   great hiss
of iron

And rain, sweet rain
Old Scratch heavy hands
parting Sista stubborn hair
'cuz everybody know
Old Sista tenderheaded
cry like she ain't got
no natural
sense

She want them fancy braids
twisting lovely in shiny rows
hair so pretty, reverse the way
Sweet River flow, Old Sista
tenderheaded but she vain
can't sit still, can't take the pain
Old Sista yelp, Old Sista holla
make Scratch so mad
he comb her harder

Now
water all up to our knees
now, water all 'round our neck
we don't welcome Old Sista tears no more
we ask the heavy hands to be still
just grease her scalp, we say
let Old Sista Sky head alone
bump her edges if you must
can't you braid no cornrows
without all that fuss?

Now, Old Scratch slick
Old Scratch mean
but he still didn't expect
this much vex

Before he dig teeth
in tender scalp
Old Sista jump up
with a shout

Before he could stomp, before he could moan
Old Sista don' up and snatch the devil comb
she beat Scratch above, beat Scratch below
they fought so long, they forgot the damn stove
hot comb burnin', hair grease smokin'
the heat turnt up too high
great blast of fire is how Sun got to Sky

So when you see the rain fallin'
but light shining bright
Remember the night
Old Scratch got whooped
by Old Sista Sky

Untitled Old Scratch Poem, featuring River

Old Scratch, soul taker
womb breaker, shapeshifter
forever playin', turnin'
his bitter tongue to sweet balm
his hailstorms to soft Wind
strokin' backs like he
know something 'bout
bein' gentle

Breeze-breezin' joy
To all he touch
But you can't trust
the wind, 'cuz Wind
play too damn much

Old Scratch think
He a mack from way, way back,
Player from the old time, the Time
Before, choosing up on a fly girl
Like me. He forget my daddy
name me River, sweetness
from God second day, can't be
Breeze-breezin' up on me
'cuz daddy didn't raise
no fool

Old Scratch think he something
Hum humming softly, wine
and sultry whispers strokin'
my bellyskin, palm palmin'
over my face and shoulders
shimmer me wet
like I don't know he sang
that same tired song to Old Sista Sky
he ought to know
I am outside to no one
afterthought to none
I let his sugar lies
drop like old stones
in the bottom of the sea
and swing my big hips
on by, on by

Bender's Bow

The covenant is broken, and there is no god.

I know this because the devil is beating his wife. The devil was beating his wife, and the bow was missing. I know this because the old woman told me. The old woman looked up at the sky, then pointed again. I followed the arc of her gaze. I looked up at the sky, through the pounding rain, but I didn't want to. I was afraid. The thunder shook my old houseboat, and I was afraid. I squinted, casting my old eyes up, searching the gray, thunderous sky. There, up in the distance I saw a rainbow. There was only a glimpse, a few lone rays peeking behind enormous rain clouds, a few rays, those damned clouds, a sky as gray and unfeeling as stone and the scent of seawater.

For a moment we did not speak, didn't mumble a word. I watched the edges of the sun shimmer faintly, the clouds drifting across the sky. I watched in silence, shivering as the old woman pointed and laughed. "Bender," she said, shaking her head of steel wool. "Bender, where yo' bow now?" She laughed, but her voice was a brittle thing, the sound of fear. It echoed across the waters, nailing me to the deck. I covered my ears, muffled the sound of her cackling. My fingers were numb from the cold. I didn't trust myself to speak, to place my heart in words that meant more in the telling, the way my little Nadja could. I looked up and knew that daylight would return, but the rains would never stop pouring.

Before us, *out there*, the water stretched beyond like something foreign, like it was incapable of cleansing or slaking thirst. The rain had started, light at first, like the sprinkle of baptism, yet steadily building, the clouds breaking and drenching the earth until nothing was left but the waters, the sky, and the few souls I fished out of that nameless sea.

The rain seeped into my rainslicker as I stood in silence, drizzled down my face, soaked my beard. The old woman was bareheaded, like the day I found her. The rain beat against her steel knots, but she didn't care. It collected in glistening black puddles at her feet. The garbage bags, the plastic ones I gave her, lay in a useless pile. She kicked them aside, sending them back toward me.

When I found her, she was all alone. I felt sorry for her, me who had no one left to feel sorry for. She was old like me. Old and useless like me, but who was I to judge her? I fished her in first, then I fished in the others—the young man and then the child.

As we stood on the deck, the wind whipped the old woman and me, made us hold our heads down like saying grace. My hands were shaking. I had worked with my hands for over thirty years in a plant, but when the rains came I wasn't sure what to do. I felt powerless, like I did the last time I hit Mariah. I felt useless like I did when Mariah lay in my arms like a limp doll, the way I felt when she never woke up again.

I picked up the garbage bags and held them close to my chest. I had poked holes in the sides of them, for the woman's arms, and one at the top for her head. She had nothing to wear when I fished her out of the waters. Like the others, she was not prepared for the rains, the rains that swallowed the whole earth up and everything in it.

Forecasters all across the country warned us about the weather, said the earth had not seen such rains since, since biblical times I guess. Most people here and around the world just shrugged, but me, I stocked up old *Mariah* like I always did, only I stuffed those cabinet shelves and that freezer with more cans and dry goods, water, and beer than they were used to. The last thing I saw before the rains came was Nadja's eyes turning away from me.

A large red "K" floated by. It looked like part of a neon sign, like the kind at a supermarket or a liquor store. I stood on the deck of the *Mariah* and watched the waves rise and fall, the big "K" swirl in the dark waters, while the old woman laughed at the sky. I pulled the hood of my raincoat closer around my face and concentrated on the brightness and shadow above. I thought about our provisions, knowing they wouldn't last, then remembered that child below. Couldn't tell what time it was, but I knew she would be waking up hungry. I took one final glimpse of the sky, then made my way back down into the cabin. Behind me the old woman stood alone in the torrent, laughing.

The man didn't like it when the old woman told tales. When she told the old stories, the ones I used to know as a young boy, he made her be silent. "Hush, old woman," Brother Brooks said. "What do you know?" The day she said the devil was beating his wife, he thought she was crazy. Only I knew that she spoke the truth. Me and perhaps the pregnant girl.

I creaked down the stairs that led to the cabin and shut the door behind me. Let the old woman dance in the rain, I thought. Let her tell her stories. What harm could they do?

Only the bulb on the ceiling lit the room, the room that used to shelter only me. Water dripped from the ceiling, sagging at its center. On the damp walls above my head hung a dull cross, the cross my poor Nadja had placed there. Beside it was a calendar dated April 13. It hadn't changed for months, since I last saw her. And the walls shuddered with each crash of thunder, the time between thunder rolls burdened with waiting. With mourning. With regret. I could feel myself slowly slipping out of time. My old body was waiting for the next world.

I stumbled past Brother Brooks asleep on the floor in the corner. I didn't like the man since the day I fished him out of that sea. He floated past me like a block of wood. Only his cry for help, a faint echo across the waters, told me that he still had life in him to breathe. He bothered me, shifty eyes and all. He bothered me, fussing about that suit of clothes and those pathetic trinkets that didn't mean much in the world anymore. I guess that's why I took to calling him Brother Brooks. He told me his name when he first arrived, but I soon forgot it. Called him Brother Brooks when he wouldn't let me peel off that suit for him. It was all wet and muddy, filled with God knows what. He wanted to fight me when I tried to take it off—and the look he gave me, like his soul had stepped out of his skin. Even while he slept I could smell fear on him. Like the old woman. Like my Nadja's poor mama, Mariah.

I called him Brother Brooks right directly, and at first he didn't like it one bit. After a while, I guess it grew on him, the way "old woman" seemed to fit that other one standing in the rain like a fool. But I could tell she was no fool. The rain had worked its own strange magic on all of us, disconnected whatever small comforts we once called home. She said she had a name, in that other life, but with the rains, it didn't mean nothing to her. The old woman took me aside when I spied Brother Brooks, the day I fished him out of the sea. She said, "I guess you've been pulled out of retirement by the Big One hisself. Guess you'll be spending your last days naming…" I sucked my teeth and went about getting Brother Brooks a brew. He didn't want it at first, asked me for a radio, something about contacting the Coast Guard. I let him make a show of trying to get someone to answer, out there in that darkness, but he soon gave that up.

When he wasn't counting the days before we would die, he counted the things he seemed to love best. From time to time he pulled his lumpy wallet out of his wrinkled suit and counted his money. He said that he had been going to be rich before the rains came. He said the rains had washed away his fortune. He unfolded the bills and counted his cash, one Ben Franklin and a few Andrews, then neatly folded them again, pressing the crease with his thumb before placing them in the wallet. Then he stared at his I.D.s and credit cards, as if he thought of charging his way out of the sea. I never noticed any children's photos or a wife's picture, even a favorite brother in those neat leather pockets.

After he grew tired of counting his money, Brooks started in on our food. He would sit on the floor, the goods lined up alongside the cabinet, his reddish eyebrows furrowed with concentration. He counted the cans and the bags and the bottles, keeping them in neat rows. When he finished, he counted them again. Sometimes he fell asleep in the middle of counting, then woke up muttering. He never said, but I guessed he might have been an accountant, a good one, too.

I crept past Brooks, past the cabinet that held our dwindling supplies. I shuffled over to the tiny bed to check on the girl. I watched her take shallow breaths, the sweat pooling near her temples. She was so young, but big-boned like my Nadja. She looked like she could be Nadja's age, no more than nineteen or twenty. Or fifteen or sixteen. Hard to tell these days. Though she was big-boned, both her arms were spindly, and her legs swollen, drawn beneath the covers and the old wedding quilt, Nadja's only gift from her mother. I tried not to think about Mariah—Mariah and her fluttering hands—as I smoothed out the heavy covers with my wrinkled fingers.

"Daddy," she said. Nearly broke my heart. It had been a long time since Nadja called me Daddy. That day

I refused to follow, the last day I saw her alive, she said, "Daddy, please come. *Daddy*, please pray with me."

I smiled at the pregnant girl, the child called Trish. When I fished her out of the sea, she had been floating, her belly swollen. She sailed through the water, along with debris, in a yellow dress, all stiff and still like a dead man. Since the coming of the rains, I'd seen too many bloated bodies. Once a child even floated past me, made me turn my eyes. It was small and bundled, the tiny arm curved out in a little wave.

When I saw Trish I was alone on deck, steering the *Mariah* aimlessly through the black waters. The old woman and Brooks were down in the cabin. I steered *Mariah* closer to the girl trying to get a better look, but the sky was the same color as the water below. I saw that yellow dress and that pregnant belly, and thought I'd better take a chance. I grabbed my rod and poked until I latched onto her dress. Then with some effort I managed to drag her to the side of the boat. By the time the old woman came up, I was climbing the row-ladder with Trish in my arms.

She groaned, making me glance at the soft curve of the covers. I watched Trish and silently wished the baby away. I knew it was wrong, felt wrong doing it, but I prayed anyway. I prayed like I did in those early days, fresh after Mariah's passing. I prayed like I did when I asked the Lord to forgive me, to help me raise my little girl like her mama wished that she could. I asked the Lord to forgive me. He never did. If my Nadja couldn't depend on me, then I didn't know what I could do for this other child.

I sat there, head bowed over Trish's bed. I thought, what if the baby didn't want to come in this weather. What if the baby didn't want to travel in this rain. The truth was that it would hurt too much to watch a baby suffer every day. The truth was I wasn't there to save my own.

I groped for Trish's hands and rubbed my hard calluses against her smooth palms, the rough texture of my fingers squeezing, trying to help her stave off the pain.

"Daddy," she said sharply, and her eyes opened quick as though to drink in a vision. She tried to sit up, but I pressed her shoulders back. She moaned and her mouth sprang open, a web of spittle caught between her lips.

I could hear the old woman outside, couldn't tell if she was still laughing or crying. "Brooks!" I shouted, startling him awake. "Get up there and get that woman. This child is fixin' to have this baby." I didn't wait to see him tear up the stairs, the cabin door bursting open and the rains pouring down on us. He came back with the old woman, and Trish started to cry. The old woman stood in the floor, squinting at me, like she was trying to clear her head. *Lord, if she tell me she don't know nothin'…*

"Move, Bender," she said, pushing me away with her pointy elbows. "What you know 'bout birthin' babies?"

I stepped away while the old woman peeled back the quilt. It tumbled onto the rain-streaked floor. The *Mariah* pitched and jerked as much as it ever had, the rain pounding my boat like the hand of God. Brother

Brooks hovered in his corner, lowered his head into his hands, wept.

⤙

The child was born with a caul over her eyes. "This is a good sign," the old woman said. No one listened to her but me. I knew the thin membrane covering the forehead and eyes meant double vision. The child might grow to be a seer—if she lived—and the gift might bring her trouble and pain if she didn't learn better. But the child was so beautiful, such a welcome sight in spite of all our misery. She had a head full of hair, dark and kinky, eyes quiet and deep like her mama's, and a little pug, shaped like a bow. I looked at her tiny feet, her small hands grasping, mouth working, and knew that at least here, in our tiny cabin, hearts still lived.

⤙

The way the boat lurched and faltered, it felt as if we were dropping off the face of the earth. Maybe the world was flat, I thought. Maybe it was so flat that we were going to drift right over the edge, like the navigators of old. There were no shorelines to speak of, few landmarks. A broken piece of signage every now and then, or some building rubble. None of it told us anything, and we never saw nobody else.

To look up and out at the sky, all that space above and below us, was to see endless water. The rain had become everything. It affected every aspect of breathing. When I did manage to sleep, with the new baby, Olivia, crying, I was pelted by rainwater, even in my dreams. The rain drowned me in my sleep. The rain drowned us all in our sleep.

One morning-night I dreamed that winds swooped down from the sky and claimed us, claimed us for the sea. We went under and no one heard from us again. It was as if we never existed. We never existed, nor the birds, the trees, the creeping things. It was a strange thing, a terrible thing to witness the birth of a new sea. It was like trying to imagine the face of God.

As the rain continued and time passed, we got used to the new baby's habits. Trish seemed to hold up well. The baby cried loud and often, like clockwork, and sometimes she was a natural chore, but I figured if little Trish could handle it, then so could we.

The old woman taught her how to breastfeed the baby, and for a while that seemed like it would be sufficient. But we soon learned that Trish needed more food to keep up her strength; the old woman and I were glad to give.

During one meal I gave the girl the lion's share of a can of peaches. She smiled at me, and it made me feel a little better, but then again, it caused me some pain. Before, I'd wondered if the girl even knew how to smile. She was so silent, always watchful. Trish had a look about her, the kind that said she knew how the flesh bruises around broken bones. Like my Mariah. Brooks jerked the can back with his mottled hands and made the girl jump. Syrup spilled in his lap. The dark stain looked like blood.

"What is wrong with you guys?" he asked. "This food can't possibly support us all."

"So what you gon' do, Brother?" the old woman asked, chewing noisily, not looking at him. "Starve the child?"

Brooks looked at the woman, the lines around her mouth looking like old scars, and from her to Trish rocking the baby, and finally to me. He passed Trish the can, not glancing at the cabinet behind her. She mumbled her thanks, and we ate in silence while the baby slept. Brooks looked shaken, as if he would take back what he had said, if he could.

⤙⤚

I imagined them throwing me out to sea. The more rain my old skin absorbed, the more comfortable I was with the idea of dying. I knew that if Nadja was there, she would have held my hand and prayed for me. But Nadja wasn't there. No, Nadja wasn't there, nor was her mama. Both were beyond my reach. Perhaps I had not completely accepted death, but I knew that it could happen. I had seen death before, reflected in Mariah's eyes. I knew that it could happen, but the knowing didn't make me less afraid, only more certain. Tired as I was, I'd never be ready to face my own.

⤙⤚

Being out here, tossed around in the dark like salt-water in a womb make you think about things you never would tell of. I was never a religious man. Nadja tried to interest me in church services, when she got old enough to go on her own, but I could never get a decent suit or rise early enough to make it to the services. She would sometimes stop by the boat and rap on the cabin door, to see if I was awake. Sometimes I pretended as if I did not hear her. Sometimes I gave her a gruff greeting, like I did that last day. She invited me to join her and the others in prayer, to pray for an end to the rains, but I gave her some lame excuse. When she tried to hug me, I hung back stiffly, gave a smile and sent her on her way—alone. She wanted me to hug her, but it didn't feel right to touch her, not with the same hands that had held her mama.

I was never a religious man, even in her mama's day, but I knew the Scriptures. The Lord gives and the Lord takes away. I had never been given much of anything, so I didn't know why I should mourn what had been taken away. But when Nadja left and the rains came, the world became smaller than I could ever have known.

⌒

The day it never stopped raining, the waters increased and bore up the ark, and lifted it up in bumps and starts far above the earth.

⌒

And there was a tree, a big one floating past. Like the one Mariah and I stood under during our first kiss. I wanted to kiss her again, but she was so shy. I kissed her hard on the mouth anyway, kissed her hard enough to leave a bruise.

It's funny, but I hated not knowing where we were drifting, as much as Brooks did. In the early days right after I retired, I would take the *Mariah* out to sea, drifting for days, sometimes weeks on end and think nothing of it. Nadja knew not to worry about me when she came to the pier and discovered me gone. I don't think it worried her none, at least not much. She knew I had done my damnedest to be there for her during all her growing years, like her mama, Mariah, would have wanted.

I wondered if the new baby would know anything other than how to walk with the sea.

I didn't want to think of death, but all around me was evidence of the impermanence of flesh. All I had to do was look in their faces.

Funny, so much water all around me, and yet my skin felt so dry.

What prevails, water or memory?

After Mariah died, after I took her life with my hands, I was no longer what I believed myself to be. Who can take a life and not be changed by the taking?

All those years I hid in my empty boat, changing.

"Kill her."

Startled, Trish clutched the baby close. Brooks' words had not come from his lips; like clouds, they had risen from the room itself, flowing from the silence, returning to it, at first everywhere—surrounding us all—then gone. Trish's eyes sought something familiar, something to remind her that we were all sane. The smooth grain on the warped, uneven floor. The cabin door and the faded calendar. While Trish studied the room, I held my breath. Reason, action, *sanity* seemed to remain beyond my reach: *out there*. Out there floating in that deep water.

Trish was hunched in the doorway of the cabin, rocking the baby in her arms on the stairs. I could see the old woman creeping slowly behind Brooks. She held an empty beer bottle in her hand. I wanted to tell her to turn back, take the children back down in the cabin, but I didn't want to alarm Brooks, didn't like that look in his eyes. From the way his knuckles whitened, I could see that he was a hair's breadth from killing. We both knew all it took was one blow to my head. One blow to the old man, and he could steer this boat wherever he would or thought he should.

Brooks looked at me with blood in the eye, but all I could think about was Mariah. How many times had I faced her with that same evil twisting my lips? My breath foul with some lifelong rage or the stink of liquor? How many times did I beat her, until there was nothing left to be broken?

Flesh bruises around broken bones.

I watched Brooks and felt my insides split. I could hardly breathe; the walls of the cabin seemed to press down on me. I stood there, unseeing, Brooks' face blurring in the dim light. For the longest time it felt like I was drowning. I remembered Mariah's face and her fluttering hands, the hands that used to slip into mine, just right, when Nadja was born. The hands that later waved me away in terror, when I flew at her, laying blame for everything I thought had gone wrong. I swayed, nausea and shame coursing through me. My throat closed up, my heart ready to explode.

I looked up. Brooks backed away from me, sobbing, tears staining his suit.

"Come here, I didn't hit you that hard." The old woman dropped the bottle and reached for him. He slumped down into her arms, let the old woman rock him. She held him, brushing away shards of glass.

I stood on the deck, tears streaming down my face, until I heard the old woman shriek.

"Trish!"

I looked up and saw the girl bolt across the deck. I could hear the baby crying through the crash of waves. Trish had left the baby bundled on the stairs and was headed overboard.

Brooks skidded, scraping a knee against unvarnished wood, trying to reach her, but Trish's yellow dress had already disappeared in the air. For a moment it seemed like time slipped, the way that yellow cloth billowed in the air. We hung over the rail, shouting her name hoarsely. At first I did not see her. Only a sliver of moon pierced the clouds, reflecting darkness above and below, the sky mirroring the water. Then I saw Trish splashing, her eyes clenched shut and arms outstretched, mouth spluttering water.

I wanted to reach out to her, but my crooked fingers couldn't grasp her hand. It was as if the muscles had forgotten the motion, the act of reaching for another. It had been so long since I reached for my own daughter. I knew if I had reached for her that day, she might have still lived. If I could have learned to reach, she would have had her mother.

Nadja and Mariah. Trish and the baby, Olivia. The feelings I had at that moment were enough to stop an old man's heart, but I knew if we didn't save that girl, there would be no reason for it to go on beating.

I heard Brooks turn and yell something at the old woman, his words swallowed up by the wind, then he disappeared from my side. I was confused, couldn't understand why he would abandon us then. Maybe he was willing to accept Trish's sacrifice, but I wasn't. I couldn't let another life slip through these hands. I climbed up on the rail, my boots slipping on the wet metal, the shrill wind in my ears. My elbows shook when I propped myself up, steadying myself to dive in, but Brooks came back and shouted for me to get down. I turned to look at him and saw that he had broken the flagpole. He charged to the rail and dangled it over the side, the stars and stripes trailing in the dark waters.

I saw Trish's head bob, then disappear under the waters. *Lord, don't let this child drown.*

"Trish!"

She came up again, flailing, before a wave swept her under. Brooks maneuvered the pole over the spot where we last saw her. For a moment it looked as if she wasn't coming up again. I could barely see, the rain poured down so. I heard the old woman and the infant wailing behind us. My heart sank at the thought of that little baby. *Please, Lord, give this child her mother.*

"There she is!" I shouted and pointed a few yards to our left. Brooks jerked the pole up, and I grabbed hold of it. I reached out with all my strength, forced the muscles in my arms to stretch, the calves of stringy legs to hold. Together we dangled it as far out as it would go. Trish was waving her hands frantically, her fingertips a few inches from the pole, but I couldn't reach her.

And then I felt the shock of icy black waters pulling me down, down into memory so deep I knew I had drowned.

⇀

The last time I saw Nadja, she turned away from me with eyes as sad as her mama's.

Lord, I wish I had reached for her then.

Lord, I can't help but wonder, if I had reached for her then, would your rains have caught us both? Caught us both on our knees praying or shifting in one of those hard mourner's pews.

Lord, I wonder sometimes. Did she reach for me, with hands just so, like her mama's?

I lay there a good spell, the rough sheets stiff against my skin before I realized that the water that was above and below now only streamed from eyes.

"Look," I heard Trish say. The child, was that the child, gurgling and giggling beside me? "He woke now. He woke."

"Well damn, it's about time!" That would be Brooks.

Somebody wiped a cool rag across my head, but not too gentle, hard, like it should have been a slap. I grunted. That would be the old woman. Steel Wool is what I'd come to think of her as. I wondered if she would ever trust us with her cradle name. Then suddenly the taste of overripe peaches filled by mouth, and I cried out, "Mariah!" My throat too raw to swallow, I spit them out, slept, dreaming of a river's roots, saltwater.

And the ark rested in the seventh month, on the seventeenth day of the month, upon the mountains… As suddenly as they started, the rains stopped.

One by one we climbed the stairs and ducked our heads out of the cabin door. A cool wind passed over us. Trish cradled Olivia and walked gingerly over to the rail. The boat creaked and rocked beneath us.

"Be careful," Brooks said as he guided the old woman by the arm. Trish turned to me and offered me the baby. Her eyes were calm assurance. I held the child with steady hands then peered over the edge, my eyes taking in the sight before us—dark rocks, twisting roots, a stretch of green and above the mountain's top, a beautiful burst of color.

"Well, Bender," the old woman sighed, looking up, "there's yo' bow."

Visitation of the Oracle at McKain Street

See them l'il girls over there? Pants all tight and
    they shoes too big?
Walkin' 'round here, lookin' like lumberjacks.
    Them l'il girls
don't know nothing about nothing. They laugh
'cause my skirt ain't on straight. They laugh
'cause my lipstick crooked,
blackberry stain all around my mouth,
mascara clumpy, raccoon eyes
like I been stumbling in the dark.
They don't know I ain't got
no mirror no more. They don't know my hand
ain't steady no more, not like it used to.
My aim ain't steady but my vision still clear.
And I see all they see and more again.

I seen the water rise. Me, who come from desert.
I seen the wild and strangeful breed rise
from Abeokuta rock, wailing across the big wata
all the way down
in them burial grounds to 125th Street,
down Beale and Congo Square.
Last night, I sat on the levee and moan.
They don't know I seen false prophets rise
centuries ago, ain't nothing new
ain't nothing in ramblin'.
I been standing on these corners

sweeping dead ends since time began
since the river I drank from turn to dust
seen them write epistles in piss
carving curses in concrete
pimping pilgrims the pastime of the ages.
I seen the newborn choke on milk poisoned.
I seen babies struggling against temptations
they ain't yet got teeth for
while you rush by me
frowning at my stink.

You don't know
this funk be spiritual
funktified force field
underneath this funk, a shield
frankincense and myrrh
guide lost spirits home.

See that girl over there? The one in the fur
knee-high boots, cussin' up storms? Like death
it's hard to escape the laughter of children.
We will meet again, but she don't know that yet.
You and I will meet again, but you don't believe
        that yet.

You don't know these mismatch clothes
cover robes that got wings.
You don't know this storefront I lean to
be the city gate of the restless.

Simeon played the fool to mock the world.
I play the damned, but you can call me saint
the big black dog guard the crossroads.

I cover the dead ends, patron of the misguided
elder of the in between.
I cover the ones that ain't got but one option left.
But if you can call me by my true name, I just
    might let you
turn around and try again.

Bottom Rock

My folk come from muddy gulches
where wildflowers grew.
Cottonmouths lived there
and snakes in other skins.
My people planted desperate seeds
afloat at the edge of stone forests.

But some rocks slip through hands
slip through the cropper's plans
the way life breaks through misery
the way love enters the world
through a woman's hips.

There is a secret
singing inside stone, sweet marrow
that holds worlds together
compresses time
in a forest—
the beginning of hunger.

My people come from bottom land
the swept floor of earth
where children grew
like trees in a boneyard.

We stand on the uneasy slope of history
heels slipping in slick mud
hungry still
but as each tree falls
new stones
labor toward air.

Lodestone, or laying the trick

—for Rushia Taylor Wade (1893-1998)

We only travel the blistering hill to follow the
    death march.
Three words, Mount Zion Baptist, carved in faded
walls, proof our people gathered there. Under
billowing sky you wipe broad hands on stiff denim.
You bend from the waist and show me how to rise
with the cotton blossoms, nurse prickly stings.
    Our rhythms
quicken, my bend more shallow despite your years.
The sky whispers a warning, your story
judgment, what the old ones mean.

I sweat before the crooked house of praise,
timber cracked, pews swollen,
funeral home fans hide behind hymnals. Life lines
    on left
palm stamp memory into dirt. Nowhere to hide
from mosquitoes, under Somerville sun,
forty-two miles from the blues. I push roots back
to strength, gather a song for the fight. Deliverance,
when the full moon comes.

Silence lives here. So quiet where you stood. It ached
like temperance. He promised you dust, candles,
    crop loans

on bottom land. You brought your own seed.
    Copper tied
to stone with string, a bribe to feed stubborn
    earth. Worked
a fierce mojo, outlived your firstborn and three
    of seven
straightbacked children—Gus and Richard,
Janie Mae, Ezekiel. One hundred and five years. You
    made hot water
bread the centuries ate. Now the house in Klondike
holds your framed baptismal scroll. The recipe bound
in Isaac's book. We only travel the blistering hill
to follow the death march. Still, the lightning sky
whispers. The field holds your secret.

Malaika Descending

I went to visit my Aunt Malaika, in Hell. The bus took so long to get there, I started to give up, tell them to let me off so I could go home. Seem like we wasn't doing nothing but driving around in circles no way, and all I could think about was *Aunt Malaika gon', Aunt Malaika gon'*. She had died about six weeks earlier, slipping on the wet pavement on her back porch and breaking her hip. They say she lay there, her wispy braids resting in her white rosebush, the thorns pushing up in her eye, until her half-blind neighbor, Miss B., looked over the fence that separated their backyards and called an ambulance.

Of course, they were late.

It took them two hours to come. "Ain't no hurry," somebody heard them say. "The old heffa already dead." I guess there was no secret about folk not liking my Aunt Laika. I can call her that now, since she gon'. She can't do nothing to me no way—not with her being in Hell and all. Because if she could, Aunt Malaika would have slapped the taste from my mouth, would have had me reciting Scriptures until I was hoarse and the black ran down my face.

Because everybody know that Aunt Ma-la-i-ka don't like nobody "skimping on her god-given syllables," messing up her melodious name. You got to say four—*Ma-la-i-ka*—or don't say it at all.

Everybody know that—at least *most* everybody.

The last time somebody messed up and called my aunt, "Miz Laika," instead of her navel name, Ma-la-i-ka, she killed them. Actually, she let their daddy die, but that's killing all the same, now isn't it? That was one of the last times somebody had to call the ambulance to Alma Street, too, and it was poor Raybone who ended up knocking on the wrong neighbor's door.

His daddy, Mr. Wilder, lived two shotguns down from my Aunt Malaika's house, on the other side of the street, and apparently Mr. Wilder had messed around and choked on a fish bone in his back kitchen. His son, Raymond "Raybone" Wilder, Jr., was staying with him again—he and his daddy had "an understanding," you see—and Raybone was so stressed out that he ran over to Aunt Malaika's house instead of calling Miss B, or Ms. Perez, or anybody, like he knew he should.

I don't know why he did this. When I think about it, it don't make no sense. He knew Aunt Malaika never liked him. Whenever she'd see him, she'd screw up her face, jaws sagging, and say, "A 35-year-old man too grown to be sitting up in his daddy's house not working," but then she'd catch Mr. Wilder, Sr., huffing down the street again, his arms filled with a grease-stained paper bag full of whatever he'd scraped up from the church kitchen, and she'd just suck her teeth and stomp back into her dusty old house.

And even her house was hateful. The high porch steps sagged and sunk like they were ready to trip any fool crazy enough to want to walk up them. The back door didn't hardly stay shut if you closed it, and that front door would mangle any key in its lock. Most days she kept her door open. No need to lock it. Nobody was desperate enough to steal from Aunt Malaika.

Later, when they asked Raybone why he didn't just call 911 from his own home, he said his daddy's phone had got cut off. I don't know about all that, but I do know that when he woke Aunt Malaika up, beating on the door like he crazy, she cussed him out and then charged him twenty-five cents for the phone call. Said that Raybone was as shiftless as his daddy, "didn't never work but always sitting somewhere, eating." Said his daddy was too big and greasy to be eating all that chicken and fried fish, anyway. And when Raybone said, "But Ms. Laika, if you don't let me make this call, he gon' be dead," Aunt Malaika started stuttering and sputtering so, that she snatched back the phone, and slammed the door in poor Raybone's face.

The ambulance came right away when Mr. Wilder died—as soon as they got the call…a good fifteen minutes later. Raybone had broke his ankle running down her evil porch steps—his big old size fifteens fell right through the floor—and he had to limp down to Mr. Denton's place to make the call. But when Aunt Malaika hit that ground on 875 Randle, on the hottest day in July, she might as well have been laying dead in the street, because by the time that ambulance come, Aunt Malaika was long gon'.

➤

Reverend Preacher say in his sermon that Mrs. Malaika Hamilton had been a fine, upstanding woman, steadfast in the Church, and didn't nobody sitting on those hard mourner's pews dare say a contrary word.

Aunt Malaika never missed a meeting of the usher board, and her white gloves and uniform were always pristine (a fine feat, given the dust she let accumulate in the house she'd been living in). Aunt Malaika had been a member of the Church longer than even the oldest deacon, and she had the dirt on damn near everyone. Still, she never would tell a soul, or at least, I don't think she would. Not many saint points in that. To Aunt Malaika, gossip was a sin. Even so, that didn't stop her from staring you down with that old knowing look in her eye that let you know that she know that you know that she could tell if she wanted to tell, and you know if you keep on backsliding, you know someday she would.

So when Reverend Preacher peered under his glasses, meeting the gaze of every one of us, we didn't do nothing but listen. "Mrs. Hamilton," Reverend Preacher say, revving up. "I said, Mrs. Ma-la-i-ka Hamilton…"

"Yes," we replied in unison.

"You know you had to get it right," Reverend Preacher say, laughing. "Sister Hamilton didn't tolerate you de-se-crat-ing her name. Sister Hamilton was a fine example to you younger folk on how to live in the fullness of the Word."

"Yes."

"I say, *the fullness*."

"Yes, Lord."

"And Mrs. Hamilton was born and raised in the *Church*," he said, clutching his Bible, "part of that noble congregation called *Old School*," and we raised our heads and said, "Amen," praying he would soon hush up, as the ushers scurried in their white padded shoes.

The doors of the church were open, but who would have thought that Aunt Malaika's soul didn't float through them.

It was true that Aunt Malaika's "steadfastness" had made her a hard soul to live with. At one point or another, everybody in the church had had some narrow dealing with her. Still, I was a little hurt, though not exactly surprised, when I got her call. Whatever happened, I never expected to see Aunt Malaika in Hell.

I don't know what I was expecting, but Hell is really small. I can hardly get my hips up in here. Despite all the fire and brimstone—you know how they say we like the heat—you can tell that Hell wasn't made for no black folk. The hallways are too narrow, and the ceiling is much too low. It keeps pressing down every time you take a step. I nearly cracked my skull trying to make my way to Aunt Malaika's raggedy room.

And the woman at the front desk just as mean and nasty—had the nerve to cut her eyes at me, like I was going to steal something.

I walked down the hall, the sulphur so thick I knew I'd be smelling it in my sleep.

Aunt Malaika shares a room with two other old women. I know this must be Hell because Aunt Malaika didn't like to share much of anything without making you feel guilty about it.

But if anyone could make a soul feel more weary in Hell, that would be Aunt Malaika. When I come in, she's sitting up on the top bunk, her fingers knotted and working in her lap, staring out a dingy window that somebody tried to cheer up with a yellow, faded crazy quilt. The stitches are all ragged and crooked, like somebody blind and shook-with-seizures sewed them. I can hardly see the pattern. I want to clear my throat, say hello, but it seems like I still can't speak in that woman's presence.

"Laika, baby, look like you got you some company."

Another old woman, clutching a photo, turns to stare at me. She wraps a tattered navy blue sweater around her thin shoulders and smiles. Her teeth are blue and stained.

"Who is it? Can't be nobody I want to see," Aunt Malaika says. "Jim-bo? Karen? Hollis?"

"No, it's me, Aunt Malaika." I nearly choke on the words, voice so quiet, she can hardly hear me. I see her turn from the window and squint.

"Who the hell is 'me'?" she asks. "Ah, don't say nothing," she says before I can answer, recognition widening her eyes. "Got to be mealy-mouthed Mildred. You the only one that bother to keep my name straight."

I nearly fall back with the force of these words.

"What you bring me, girl, 'cause the food up in here ain't fit to feed a snake."

I hold out my palms, sweating.

She looks disgusted.

I could have kicked my own butt for coming empty-handed, but hell, what a body supposed to bring to a woman that swear she don't need anything? I'd been trying to figure out how to please this woman since before I was born, and from the frown on her face, I guess she was going to keep me trying now that she done worried herself into Hell.

She brushed back her braids with the back of her hand and pulled a yellow cardigan over her ample breasts.

"Don't mind this," she said when she caught me staring. She tugged the *I'm Retired-What's Your Excuse?* T-shirt self-consciously. "It's too hot to be walking round here in all that mess. I don't know what made your Cousin Hollis dress me in that awful, gaudy red dress. Knowing full well I wouldn't be caught out in no hussy slip like that." "It was pink, not red," I said, "and I thought you looked nice, Aunt Lai…Malaika."

"You *would*," she said, narrowing her eyes at my flouncy sundress.

I was never her favorite niece.

She leaned forward, grabbing my wrist, and hissed in my ear.

"What you say, Aunt Malaika?" I could barely understand her. Her breath smelled like Juicy Fruit and Denture Klean.

"I said, don't you eat nothing up in here," she whispered loudly. "Don't eat a crumb or a cracker, and watch out for that heffa at the front desk. She sneaky. She'll mess around and have you singing a blues for every season."

"Okay, Aunt Malaika," I said slowly, like I understood. This heat and sulphur must have fried up her poor brain.

"You best to listen to your Grandmama," the plump one says. She was sitting in one of those green plastic deck chairs, her flowery duster spread out across her

54

thick thighs. She'd been staring at a muted TV screen that was mounted in a corner of the wall. A skein of orange tangled yarn rested in her lap. I watched her pale grey eyes return to the black and white stories on the tube. The other one sat beside a faded chiffarobe, the vanity table cluttered with warped and peeling photos of children, smiling and gap-toothed. They stared back at me, making me think of ice cream and pulpy lemonade, the kind the other—"wayward"—kids used to get when I was sweating in Sunday school.

"That your grandbaby?" she asked.

"I told you she ain't," Aunt Malaika barked, gritting her teeth. "I ain't never had no children, and ain't never wished I could."

I clasped my hand, nails biting into the palm flesh. Before I came, I said I was going to be nice to Aunt Malaika, like I always have, but she was testing me. Though nobody could ever say I wasn't grateful for how she took me in and raised me like her own, I never much cared for the way she had of not claiming me. No, I wasn't her natural born, but she was the closest thing to a mama I'd ever known. And if I wasn't her daughter, I might as well be, because all the other kids, *Cousin Hollis* included, was scared of her and wouldn't have nothing to do with her.

That's probably why Hollis buried her in that red dress.

I decided to change the subject.

"So how you settling in, Aunt Malaika?"

She looked at me like I had lost my mind. "Well what you think?" she asked. "One minute I'm minding my business, watering my rosebush—you know how they get during the summer—and the next, I'm trying to raise my head to meet My Maker. I look up and find myself in this Hellhole, and ain't a real rosebush the first or a drop of air conditioning here."

I look at her in disbelief.

"That's why I ain't never wanted no public assistance," she continued. "They'll welfare you right out of a good house and into the state penitentiary. It's too hot up in here, and I been trying to tell that old battle axe up at the front desk, but she don't listen. Talking 'bout 'take it to Jesus…'"

"I'm so sorry," I say, a little breathless. I'm starting to see what she means. I can hardly breathe myself, and I feel my sundress clinging to me, hot and sticky against my skin. "Why don't I open this window for you," I say, pulling back the curtain.

"It's *stuck*," she says, rolling her eyes.

No, she never liked me, even though I was the only one who bothered to see about her. But I couldn't help myself. I wanted to fight it off, but here I was again, trying to prove my worthiness. I tugged harder on the window pane, trying to force it up with the tips of my fingers. It didn't budge, but I did see a sight that made me still and queasy.

The window was nailed shut, big red rusting nails driven deep into the window sill. But just beyond it was a rosebush, so big and beautiful, perfectly rounded with its soft petals and luscious leaves gleaming like God's Great Own, like something straight out of Eden.

No wonder Aunt Malaika stayed glued to that window.

That's when I started wondering what Old Grey Eyes was missing in that TV, and Miss Thin—what kind of a sad story was hidden behind those children's gap-toothed smiles and eyes?

I keep staring at the rosebush until it moves. I think it moves, or maybe that was just—

A thorny branch snakes up and hisses at me, then slams hard into the window pane, cracking the glass. An odor begins to fill the room, so foul and thick that Miss Thin begins to wail.

"Baby, just shut it," Aunt Malaika says, waving at the curtains. "Shut it quick before I have to listen to Velma all day." Her voice is tired, almost resigned. I have never heard Aunt Laika sound this way.

I yank back the tattered curtains, listening for the next assault, but the rosebush soon tires and slinks back into itself. The room is quiet, silence falls around us like a heavy shawl. Below the ragged calm of Miss Thin's breathing, I hear the low-voiced hum of distant climate control. Perhaps a heater.

Miss Thin slumps in her vanity chair, the pictures tumbling over in their gilded frames. Grey Eyes falls back into the rhythm of her voiceless stars, their movements a slow pantomime against the colorless screen.

I sit next to Aunt Malaika, my knee pressed against her thigh, and stare at the hidden window. Aunt Malaika loved her rosebush. She prized its roots more than any sour fruit on her swaybacked peach trees. Before the sun rose, she was out with her rusty watering can in hand. And three times each day, before it set, she would water it again, sprinkling it from her cupped hands, as if it was her own backporch baptism.

When I was a child, I used to watch her from my bedroom window. These quiet times, when dayclean was just bending into daydone, she chose to be alone. She never let me help her, afraid that I might pour too much or crush the delicate petals and leaves with my eager hands. But she let me watch, and for that I was grateful. Her rosebush was the only thing of beauty she allowed in her yard.

"Remember how you used to wipe my eyes with rose petals, after you bathed me and put me to bed?" I say suddenly. "Your rosebush had a special scent. I ain't smelled it in years, but look like I woke up the other day and heard you call my name."

"How you remember a thing like that?" she says.

She gives me another look, not so long, not so knowing, then scratches her scalp, flicking dandruff from a white braid. For the first time, I imagine the young girl in her, what she must have looked like when she was close to my age. She still has that head of hair all the other usher mothers envied. I look around. I don't see any mirrors. I guess you don't need none in Hell. I wonder if she knows.

"When I was a youngun, not such a slip as you, but young enough," she begins, "them old mothers used to say a night bath in rosewater kept a girl's future soft and sweet. Something 'bout sealing a woman's ways."

I laugh. "That *is* sweet."

She grunts. "Oh, that ain't nothing but some hoo-doo mess, them old ways from folk that don't know no better. You feeling mighty 'soft and sweet' now?"

I *was,* I want to say, *'til you got ugly.*

"That your grandbaby?" Miss Thin asks again. It's like her mind is one of those old phonographs, and she's stuck on the same groove. She's fondling her framed pictures, smiling, spittle hanging from her lip. Aunt Malaika frowns and shifts on the bed. "No, Velma, that's my daughter. How old you think I is, anyway?"

I don't say nothing, just look at Aunt Malaika.

"Well, what her name? You been sitting over there whispering and ain't introduced nobody."

"Her name Hollis…"

"—Mildred," I mutter.

"Mildred," she continues, not missing a beat, "has come to visit me, and we was talking, *minding our business,*" she adds with emphasis. It occurs to me that Aunt Malaika is possessive of a visitor, even me. This is gratifying, and I can hardly contain my smile.

"Well, Mildred, welcome to Hell, child," Miss Thin says, brightly. "I know it ain't what you thought it was, but we gon' do our best to make you enjoy your stay. You must have done something mighty bad, though, something sinful to come down here, but I can't tell what it is, sweet as you seem to be. But you never know…they don't tell you nothing. Just sign you in and lock you up."

"Never know?" Grey Eyes snapped to attention, her head pivoting away from the TV screen. "What you mean 'you never know?' What somebody got to tell you 'bout yourself that you don't already know? You here the same reason why we all here."

"And what's that?" Miss Thin say, her eyes darting round the room.

"'Cause you triflin'. You was triflin' when you was living and now you triflin' in death."

"I *ain't* triflin'!" Miss Thin yell, banging her tiny fists on her gilded keepsake chest. "Is it wrong to want a little bit of loving for yourself? Is it wrong to want somebody just for you?"

"That's the problem. He wasn't for you. He was *married,* and all them children you doting on, sitting on that desk, ain't got no part of you in them. They his, and his alone." She paused, doubled back. "Naw, that ain't right. They his—*and his wife's.*"

"It ain't true," Miss Thin says, her eyes pleading with me. I knot the hem of my dress, fingers working, nervous—same thing I did when I was child. I don't want to hear this. In fact, I want to go.

"And if you had the backbone enough to love a married man, you should have had backbone enough to love your ownself!"

"Stop it, Gladys," Aunt Malaika says. "That's enough from you."

"Yeah," Miss Thin says, between sobs. "We not gon' talk about why you here, now are we?"

"No, we're not," Aunt Malaika says, severely. "Seem like you two would get tired of fussing and fighting. Ain't none of us going nowhere."

"Well, at least we have this nice young thing to keep us company," Miss Thin says, perking up.

"Velma, she ain't here to stay. She just visiting, and in fact, she 'bout to go," Aunt Malaika says, struggling to stand up. Baffled, I hold her by her elbow, and let her lean on my shoulder as she gets to her feet. She's reaching a bare toe across the floor, looking for her slippers. "Come on child," she said, hurried. "Wouldn't want you to miss your bus."

"But Aunt Malaika, I just got here, and we ain't hardly talked," I say as she dusts me off and straightens my loose shoulder strap. Suddenly, I feel like the floor been swept from underneath me. Why she rushing me out now?

"Mildred, we done said all that we need to say. You look good, so I guess, hard as it was, I done good," she says, brushing her hard knuckles against my cheek. She looks at me with something I've never seen from her before: satisfaction. "You always was a good child, but so scared of stepping on your own shadow, I couldn't hardly get you to stand on your own feet." She stared up into my face, searching. "But you standing now, ain't you? And now you must go. Visiting hours should be just about up."

"Well, if you don't want her to stay, you better get her out of here," Gladys says. "'Cause when that heffa come with those pills…"

Aunt Malaika sighs. "I know." She turns to me. "Come on, Mildred, give your mama a kiss."

I look at her, feeling both guilt and relief. I move to the door, hurriedly, before her mood changes—or she changes her mind. I'm her daughter. That's what she said. No turning back from that. She satisfied.

"Should I come back, some time next week? Next Sunday?"

She pats a loose braid and places it smoothly behind her ear. Her fingers have a marked tremor. We have the exact same ears, shaped like little rose petals. Why didn't I notice that before?

She looks troubled. "Baby, if you like. But you got to go now. And Mildred…"

"Yes?" I say, standing at the door.

She reaches out, and for a moment, I think she will hug me, but she grasps my wrists. Her hands are cold—deadly cold. "Don't look behind you," she says, staring at me until I understand. "Remember."

Forget what they tell you. Hell is very small, and crowded. The ceilings are low and the hallways are narrow. A full-bodied soul like me can't hardly make no elbow room. And the air, the air smells like pot liquor and cooking grease, like something holed up in a smoky kitchen.

I walk quickly through the winding corridors, the ceiling getting lower and lower, like some kind of strange limbo. Eyes averted, my hands resting at my sides, I am not holding back tears. I am not thinking of my Aunt Malaika sitting on her bunk bed by a wavering window, staring at a strip of green, receding. I am not concentrating on white roses, sharp elbows resting in a dusty windowsill. I am not thinking of my mother. And I don't look back.

Dust

A woman sits on a porch of weathered board
her skin the texture of the dried apple dolls
grandmamas gave children years ago.
When asked about the past, she will not speak—
only four words that peel back history
Them time was hard.

Her hands have worked iron
fashioned each bit into the tools
that make a home, axes and shovels
hinges and locks, gates and railings
skillets and chains, a harness
shaped by hands that gripped metal
as lungs grip air, grip breath
hands that could not protect
her or any of her children.

If she speaks, she might break apart
scattered like so many bits of iron
hot embers cooling in the wind
luminous as fireflies, the dust of her
flying across the backs of stooped men—
two brothers, an uncle, a dead husband
chained by their debt to the fields.

Evening wears into night. The stars
gather like sisters, a shawl round her shoulder.
She presses both lips together, then groans
the oldest language our land knows.

Touch

Ms. Ci-ce-ly, that's what she call me. Say it like there's a bunch of zee's in my name. I like the way she do. Make it sound important, like the name come from somewhere you want to be. She call me and I fix her something light to eat. Give her a glass of cool water and sit down next to her, nod my head while she talk. That's all we do. She talk and I listen. Wipe the crumbs from her face, if she let me. She funny about touch, don't like nobody to hardly deal with her. Say she can't stand the feel of other folk flesh against her skin. Don't bother me none, not at all, 'cause when she talk, I like to listen, but I don't let her know. She say the oddest things, that she do.

Like that first time she tell me her people come from water. Didn't know what she meant by that, so I asked her.

"Come from where?" I say. "What water? You talking 'bout somewhere in Europe?" A lot of these white folk talk about the "old country," even if they ain't never been nowhere near it. Farthest I been is to see my grandniece in Evanston, but Ms. Rowan shake her head, no. I tell her my people come from Mississippi, maybe that muddy water was what she had in mind. She shake her head again, wave her arms, slow-like—big swooshing motion. "Bigger?" She nod, yes. "Oh," I say.

"Your people stay near the ocean." Wrong again. I raise her up, plump the pillow beneath her neck. Blue lines stretch all 'cross her skin, like water through her veins. "Bigger," I say. "Bigger than the ocean? I don't know no body of water much bigger than that."

And that's when she smile at me, gray eyes sparkling 'til they start to look green. Then I wonder what she looked like before the years started pulling at the skin around her neck and jaws and her eyes. Mine starting to look like that, too, like my body starting to forget itself, like the skin don't remember how to hold onto bone, but I'm my mama's daughter. Be a while 'fore it's full-blown. You know, it ain't true what they say. Black do crack—it just take its time doing it.

I look at Ms. Rowan's head, gray roots leaning back into red, like her ends been touched by the sun, but it's only Miss Clairol. The agency say she sixty-nine, but I know better. She look back at me and smile. Might have been pretty once, way back when. Can't tell now though, 'cause she don't have no pictures in the house, not like natural folk do, not a one. In my time, I have took care of quite a few elders, folk they loved ones remember and some they forget. It get me worried sometime. I don't want to be sitting up in nobody's old folk home, eating Jell-O and unsweetened Kool-Aid, fretting away 'cause I'm lonesome. I may not have no children, but I do have kin. Hoping somebody will be around to look after me, if it do come to that.

But Ms. Rowan don't have nobody. Nobody, unless you count all them statues and knickknacks of bugs she got hanging everywhere. Thangs hanging all over the house, sitting up on her bookshelves and side tables, hanging from expensive, heavy frames on the wall. Water beetles, that's what she call them. No, scarabs. Look like cockroaches to me. She laugh when I say that. Sound like the wind blowing through an old bent tree. That's Ms. Rowan. She can go days without saying nothing, then when she get started, seem like she never gon' quit.

"As nice a place this is," I tell her, "why you want to be sitting up 'round all these nasty bugs? Don't they scare you?"

"Not bugs," she say, eyes beetling at me like a spider. "Family. And family is where you first learn fear."

She worry me when she start with that oddness. Loving a bug is one thing; calling it your kin is another. And fear in the family. Don't even get me started. Now, I like to collect thangs, too, much as the next. I like sunflowers, real pretty bright ones, the kind where the petals look like bonnets. I got me some china dishes with sunflowers painted all over them, and my rugs and my towels and things like that got the same sunflower print. I got sunflowers all in my house but can't get none to grow in my yard. But that's alright though. My little shotgun is not as decked out as all this, but if it was, I'd fill it with flowers, not no nasty bugs. Ms. Rowan's got one of those three-stories in Midtown, near the park, built back when there wasn't nobody but white folks in North Memphis, them and all they Confederate kin. Statues stashed all over the place like they some kinda Dixie memorial. Now these old houses are bordered up by the 'hood. And there's all kind folk living there would love to have as much room as this to walk through, stretch they legs a bit.

I tell Ms. Rowan this, but she don't listen. Or she do and keep doing the same, which is nothing. Sitting and staring, laying in that bed, talking nonsense. Scratching her arms, big long scars that don't never seem to heal up, talking 'bout, *where my wings*. You know how old folk do. Set in their ways. This her house, I keep telling myself, and I ain't got to live in it. I have to tell myself this every time I mess around and stumble on one of them bugs she like to caress, holding and stroking them, calling them out by name like they kin and friend. Just come through three days out of seven, dust up some, shake a few pans and some sheets, cook her up a mess of meals, and listen to her talk about her *family*. She mad 'bout them bugs, convinced they as good as people, love them more than anybody out in the street. Ain't never heard her say different.

What kind of mess is this?

The other day she asked me to get her uncle from the top shelf.

"Your uncle? Ms. Rowan, I ain't got time for this today. I got laundry to do, and you claim you want some hot cakes—from scratch. Hot cakes for lunch, hot as it is, and I ain't never heard of such…"

"I'm getting so dry," she say. "I need water…"

I look at her real close. Do seem like her skin kind of parched. Them scars kind of scab up. Her lips chapped a bit, something awful really, like she ain't had a drop of water in days. And if she had have been a sister, she would have been ashy, would have needed a whole pot of Vaseline to fix her up, but she all splotchy

splotchy—you know how some of them get—look like she 'bout to peel off and hit the floor.

She keep grumbling and I shake my head. She don't look so good.

"Ocean?" I say, frowning. "I can't hardly tell where you from with that accent. What you gon' do with the ocean? Too much salt in it, you can't drink it. 'sides, I just brought you three glasses of water. How much water can a soul drank?"

She smile then, real funny like she remember an old joke.

"Don't drink water," she say. "Breathe it. Give me another glass, Cicely. I can't feel my wings."

"Ms. Rowan, you ain't gon' worry me today," but I put the linen down and go get her glass. She drink it greedily, hands trembling, eyes closed so tight would have thought she just dragged up out the desert. I let her hold on to the tumbler and consider giving her the pitcher. *No, don't nobody need that much water, I don't care how thirsty they is.* I wipe the yellow counter down, careful not to knock one of her knick knacks on the floor. These bugs sho' starting to worry me. Look like she got more stashed 'round the house than the last time I was here. I pick up one, wrinkling my nose. It don't smell bad, just a faint hint of alcohol or something, and it's shiny, like it's been covered in varnish. Its blue body sparkles and gleams in the afternoon sun peaking through the kitchen window. The other one is a dark green, with bits of orange and a big ole mouth shaped like a can opener. Why she want these thangs sitting up in her kitchen, of all places, I'll never know. That's why she ain't got no company.

She can't stand for me to talk too bad 'bout them, get all hincty. The first time the agency sent me over and I tried to throw out some of the real ugly, dusty ones, she liked to have a fit. "Leave them be," she say, eyes so narrow and squinty I thought they had sunk right back in her head. "And I never call you out your name, so you'd do well not to bad-talk my people." *Her people?* Child please! If my niece hadn't messed around and got herself another baby, I would've told the agency they could kiss my natural ass. Between this and my other overnight jobs they got me rotating, I can just barely keep my house payments up and send a little extra to Laqueshia and n'em in Illinois. She keep talking 'bout she gon' visit, but I know she just talking. I might have to take some leave and go on up there to see 'bout her and that baby.

They came and took Ms. Rowan last night. Got her 'round midnight. Neighbors say they took her from her bed and didn't even change her nightclothes. Just dragged her to the ambulance and dumped her at the Home. When I got to her house the next morning, she was gone, and it don't look like she took any of her bugs with her.

It took me a while to work my nerves up enough to go see her. Last time I was in a home like that, it was to see my own grandmama, and the way she looked at me when I left her there made me never want to come back again. Don't seem right to live your life right, only to end up holed up in one of them old folk farms, put out to pasture. Ms. Rowan had more grit than anybody

I know, but I couldn't rightly tell how she might make out in a state home.

When I went to see her, the child at the front desk made me wait outside for forty minutes. Sound like she wasn't doing nothing but talking to her boyfriend or somebody, but when I ask her what's the trouble, she start shuffling paper like she busy. And when I finally did get to Ms. Rowan's room, it took me a minute to catch my breath. They had her dressed in work overalls, with her room and bed number stenciled on the front, name of the unit on the back. *Getwell Gardens*, please. One of those trapdoors low on the bottom, I guess for easy access. When I come to the bed, she wouldn't even speak to me. Look like her gray eyes carry blame, they so dark they flint. But how was I supposed to know they'd take her so quickly? Thought I was slick coming through there, tidying up like I always did, fixing her food, and listening, always listening to her water tales of bug life, even after the agency sent that last warning. How was I supposed to know they'd get through her paperwork so quickly? As many cases they got, seem like it would have took longer 'fore they realized that my assignment was long overdue. But they run the Homes like they do everything else in this city. If you can't pay, can't nobody but God help you. Budget crisis got them cutting every corner. No room in the inn, they just pat you down and sign you off into the ward.

Don't nobody leave.

Break my heart. I don't want my last days spent in no dirty diapers and oversized overhauls, in a cold, unfamiliar room, touched by strangers.

"Ms. Rowan?"

She don't answer at first. Just laying in that little hard bed, the pillow so flat she probably got a crook in her neck. I put my bag down and pull a chair to her bedside.

"Ms. Rowan, it's me. Cicely." Her eyes are closed, but I see her lids flicker a bit. The skin so thin and dry, it sounds like the pages of a book turning. "What they got you in here doing? Breaking the law? Up to no good?" I try to get her to laugh, but she won't acknowledge me, so I sit still a minute, letting my eyes take in this piece of a room.

She had one window with no view. It looked over the roof of the complex, and from what I could tell, look like a new group of inmates were coming in a van. Could have been a death car, far as they were concerned, 'cause I could tell from the plastic flowers, the shabby chair, and the lumpy rug centered in the room, they didn't expect much company here and made no effort to sweeten these folk's lives. All I could do was shake my head and try to sound cheerful.

"Ms. Rowan, I brought you something."

Her eyelids flickered a bit, trembling like thin paper. "I don't know what they been feeding you in here, and finicky as you is, I 'spect you ain't eating no matter what it is. But fix your lips for this!" I waved a big slice of potato pie before her, hoping she'd stop playing sleep and rise up a bit.

"Come on, Ms. Rowan, you know I don't be playing with my sweet potato pie. Not everybody get this gift I'm laying on you."

Then I hear it, sound like a dry husk, cicada skin in the wind. "Ci-ce-ly," she say, like her chords rusted in her throat, her lips so chapped, she don't say *water;* she say it like this, *"wata."* I hold the pie a moment, feeling stupid, then wrap it back up in the aluminum foil, place it on the side table. "Ms. Rowan, what they don' done to you?"

She straining a moment, chest heaving slow, her face pained; then I see why. There's just enough light in the room for me to see the slow tear ease down the wrinkles in her face, her skin so dry, don't even look like she got enough *wata* in her to make no tears.

Lord, why did I think some pie was gon' cheer her up?

After my eyes don' took in nearly every inch of the room, the tow-down faded curtains, the mismatch furniture, and the empty Tupperware pitcher, I scoot my chair closer to her, forcing myself to really see her.

Now, I could be wrong, but I don't believe Ms. Rowan wasn't never no beauty queen, still she had an order about her that made you respect what God give her all the same. But it's clear from the dry patches on her jaw and chin that she ain't been herself since she come here. Ms. Rowan hair all disheveled like it ain't been touched in ages. I dig in my purse to see if I brought a comb. I push aside an old pay stub, come up with a nail clipper and a few sticks of Big Red, but no comb. I put the bobby pins on the side table and see what I can do with my fingers, cramped as they is.

Ms. Rowan don't move away when I reach for her, so I know she feeling bad. Her hair feels thin, lifeless. There ain't but a touch of Clairol left, faded crimson on her brittle ends. Her scalp all scabby, like all her hair 'bout to fall out, and I brush away little flakes that disappear in my hand. She smell funny, too, but not like that Ajax and lemons the Home use to keep the piss smell from drifting in the hall, not musk or sweat either, but an iron scent, copper like blood or some strange metal, something I ain't never smelled before.

"When the last time they wash yo' hair?" I say and laugh to keep from crying. Her eyelids flicker but she don't answer. She turn her head a little, closer to me. *That's better*, I think. "Somebody got to clip your ends. Wish I'd thought to bring my comb," I say as I struggle with a knot, parting the hair with my fingers and twisting her stringy strands into a cornrow, tight like the way my grandmama used to do me.

Ms. Rowan lay there, still as silence. I sing a hymn while I twist an end, then gently lay the braid over her shoulder. "Now that's pretty," I say, pleased, though the part's not as straight as it could be. Just when I'm thinking I'd better leave, her hands clamp my wrist.

"Cicely," she say, holding my wrist so tight. I want to pull away. "I come from the *wata,* the *wata* is the cradle, the *wata* is my birth. My people come from the *wata*, ancient breed of life. I come from the river, the one you call Mississippi, but I ain't the last, just the last 'round here. My people the first life, the first that come on the planet. For us, all *wata,* all bugs is sacred. The *wata* hold us, the life force of this planet. Though most fear, I am not, we are not, your enemy."

She squeezing me, talking so fast, that iron scent all 'round me.

"I have lived millennia," she say, rising up, her pointy elbow digging in her bed sheet, "never far from the *wata,* never far from the source. But Cicely, this body growing weak. I need *wata.*"

I don't know what to make of all that. Sound like she don' lost all her natural mind. But even crazy folk deserve they dignity; it don't make no sense to have nobody living like this.

"Ms. Rowan, don't you got no people I can call?"

She look at me, her face all slack, eyes narrowing, like I'm the dumbest child in the room. She look at me like I ain't heard a word she said, she look at me and say "*wata*!" then point to the bathroom.

She struggling to get up, so I push back my chair, return to home-aide mode. This is what I know how to do. I let her lean against me as she trembles, trying to stand, that's when I see her feet. The poor thing's nails ain't been clipped, her heels are ashy, and I didn't have but a sample size of shea butter when she need a whole pot of grease.

"Steady now," I say, but she feel like air in my hands. Her bones so thin, I wouldn't be surprised if I could see Adam's rib. We take our time getting 'cross the floor, and she holding on me tight, raspy breathing in my ear. Not breathing, humming, hymnlike, "*wata, wata,*" over and over again, like a prayer.

When I peel her overalls off, I nearly drop her. Her body is covered in this thick, clear squooshy stuff, like baby oil gel, but it smell like iron, and it take all I got not to just put her in the tub and leave. Let them Home folk deal with it. But that ain't my nature, and the State don't care no way.

74

I sit her in the tub, in that stall that look like a big high chair, take a sponge and the little bit of hard black soap that's more like brine. I wash her back, gentle as I can, but when the sponge come up, I see it's covered in a layer of skin. I search, but she not bleeding nowhere, steady humming, like it feel good. I don't know how long I keep this up before I get her all cleaned. The water look funny, yellow at first, then kinda sparkly, then I wrap her in a towel, dry off her, and lead her back to the chair. Her eyes seem brighter now, she watching me as I strip the stained sheets from her bed. I pull a clean set from a dresser, make up her bed, carry her in my arms, she holding tight like she carrying me.

"You need anything?" I ask, reaching for my purse. I flick a ladybug from my wrist and hoist the bag over my shoulder. "I'll be back, maybe early next week."

She look at me hard, like she know the truth ain't in me, but don't say nothing, just lay there, playing sleep.

I am almost out the door, when her steady voice stop me.

"Cicely," she say, "do this for me…"

Can't believe I'm out here digging in the garbage.

Work all my life, sometime two, three jobs, since I was seventeen, and here I am, *still* a bag lady. Ms. Rowan better be glad I call myself a Christian, even though I don't show up at church but twice a year. Better be glad, 'cause had it been for anybody else, them thangs would've still been sitting in the street.

I come to the house early this morning, thinking I'd get here before anybody I know see me, but don't you know the City don' already throwed all her stuff out, got it sitting up in black garbage bags on the curb. I would've knocked on the door, just to see who they got up in there now, but I wanted to get this mess and be gone, so I can get back home and fix me something to eat before my next shift.

Now I wasn't in the door good, before that little girl at the front desk stop me.

"You've come to see 3WRWP60?" she say, staring at me like I stole something,

"What?"

"The client on the third floor, in Permanent housing?"

"Ms. Rowan? Yes, I'm Ms. Harris, I come to see 'bout her. Why?"

She purse her lip and speak real slow, like I'm three years old. "Well, Ms. Harris, we wondered if you could speak with her. There have been," she paused, "problems."

"What kinda problems?" I ask, suspicious. They better not start nothing up in here, because I can't do nothing with Ms. Rowan. I stare at the girl's pass key, see her name is Aminata.

"After you left, we found her wandering in the grounds."

I take this in, trying to figure out how Ms. Rowan get the strength to walk anywhere, as bad a shape she in. How you lose some old folk, anyway? But it's clear these folk in the Home don't pay nobody no attention.

"Well, how she get there?"

The girl don't answer. Keep talking like she ain't just heard me speak. "Ms. Harris, if she keeps breaking curfew, we will have to reassign her." She stares at me, and I know what that means.

"Is that all?" I ask. This ain't a train of thought I want to follow.

She stop, like she trying to think of what *not* to say. "There is just one thing."

"Yeah?"

"She refuses to eat. The aides say she has refused all of her meals for a whole week."

She motions for an aide, and he brings me a tray. I take a look under the cover and sigh, don't look like nothing a starving man would want to eat. I hug my purse close to me and balance the tray as the aide opens the door.

"You know, ma'am, she don't give us no trouble," he says, loud whispering like he ain't used to being heard. His gray uniform is neat, and I see somebody taught him to press his slacks, polish his shoes. Nice young man, look like he got home training. "She just keep getting up and walking. They mad 'cause don't nobody know how she get out. When we found her, she was standing in the fountain, fully dressed." He give me a look like he want to say more, then as he close the door, "My grandmama stayed here, too."

I thank him, not sure what to say to that and like to drop the tray when I come through. Ms. Rowan sitting up in that bed, damn near blacker than me. If I didn't know better I would have thought that she'd been down in Miami sunbathing.

"Well, where *you* been?" I ask, putting the tray down, hoping I can get her to laugh. But when I sit down beside her, the joke catch in my throat. It ain't just that her skin don' tanned, practically like we could be kin, but it's all scaly, like there's a thin web just under the skin. I try not to let the shock takeover my face, but it's hard.

"Ms. Rowan, you ain't looking like yourself."

She wait a minute, throw her head way back and holler, the laughter womb deep.

"Cicely," she say, her voice so low. I got to lean in close to make my ear reach.

She wipe a tear from her eye, say, "You ain't stopping no men in the street either."

Dang if she ain't still salty. I plop my purse on the table and dig 'round, like I'm mad. "Here," I say and hand her the green glass beetle. It's the only one in all the bags that wasn't smashed up or half broken, and now I'm ready to leave.

"Look, I don't know what you been doing, but whatever it is, you need to stop. These folk don't play with you here. If the Home transfer you to Mental, there ain't nothing else I can do. Ain't no visitors there and well, truth is," I say, looking down, "I don't rightly know what else I *can* do."

I look back up, but she ain't paying me no mind. She holding that dang beetle, her *kinfolk*, like it is the Hope diamond.

"Ms. Rowan," I say, but her fingers working, stroking its glossy green back, its long wings. I stand up and zip my bag and try not to grieve. "I'll be back," I say, "but maybe not next week. I'll be back, okay?"

She don't say nothing when I leave.

✦

The next time I come she gone.

A white-haired man, turned on his side, snoring like grizzlies. I guess that's his family over there, trying to convince themselves to hang 'round 'til he wake up and not slink out like thieves.

"And that ain't my daddy," his son say, crying, the woman at his side, making calm-down motions, rubbing the small of his back like he the baby. "The lips, the eyes, the shape of his head, the cheeks don't favor him."

I stand in the doorway, turning to leave when the baby, cutest thang, dressed in a blue jumpsuit, tear away from his father's grasp. "Ooh, bub!" he cries as he run to stand before the window.

Ladybugs, hundreds of them, orange and red with speckled backs covered the glass, a bright, wavering ribbon.

The water is cold.

"Mama CeCe?"

Sound like somebody calling my name from far away. I open my eyes and find my fingers and toes all wrinkly.

"How long I been sitting in this tub, child?"

Laqueshia shrug her shoulders, "I dunno," she say and hand me my robe.

"Where Buba at?"

"We going to the backyard."

"Alright, I'll see you there."

I put my house dress on and head out back. I can hear Buba squealing before the screen door shut.

"Whatchu doing out here?" I say before I see the other child.

She standing in my yard, near my sunflowers, Buba pulling up weeds, laughing and giggling at her feet.

"Where you come from, child?" I ask. Laqueshia just shake her head. The girl is a long-legged, redheaded thing, no more than four or five, with gray eyes glimmering so, in the fading light they almost look green.

She holds a wild dandelion, blows, the seedlings fly off in the breeze. Up, up, and up again. She smiles at me, waiting. Her skin is luminous and smooth, clear as water.

"Ms. Rowan?" I say, bending so low, I feel the ache pull at my knees.

The sun is fading fast. Mosquito's buzz, gnat's whine fill the darkening air. A breeze kicks up from the east, and grandmama's willow tree seems to lean in close to listen. The child looks at me, her mouth full of bees, zees, recognition in her eyes, says "Ci-ce-ly."

She raises tiny clenched fists and stares expectantly.

Unsure, I point to the right. She shakes her head no, impish grin.

I point to the left, Buba giggles, crawling to her mama on little square knees.

The red child don't speak, but thrusts her open palm at me. An emerald beetle with long silvery wings rests in the palm of her unlined hand.

"Touch," she say and smiles at me.

Lightning bug reflects a mason jar of silence—gold dust in my hand.

Sky in West Memphis

on this night
we swat mosquitoes
eat falling stars
before they reach the earth
your love is silver
caught in my throat

Djarkarta rising...

epiphany at Djarkarta

impossible landing
beyond Ibo
too late to turn back
and fly away...

what ground is this
what god is honored here
we have wandered
far beyond our mother's breast
push aside particles of light and air
between our sight and this vision
and pray that what we seek
is worth this running

under a brackish sky
of doubled moons
before that last copper-edged eclipse
ears strain before the bang end of our world
we hear something dark and prayerful
in a language more actual than speech

in this life
the surest failure
is the unattempted

Jigganaut

When Mama say, I dance. I press my toe in Uncle Bo Bo's shoe and jump and bow, the ole jim crow. When Mama say, *reel*, I reel. I leap and squat, turn and stop, flap my arms way up like a chicken. Mama take the black soot and rub it all over my face. Mama take the black soot and smear it cross my chin. It feel cold at first, cold like the air outside our window, then it warm up when I sweat. Mama say I can fan my hands and wave and wave at the people laughing, but I can't wipe my face, can't scratch my face, no matter how much the black soot itch. Mama don't want nobody to see the black of my skin. She say, the black God give us ain't good enough. She say, the folk outside don't want to see real black, they want to see ole black, ole joe black.

I don't know who Joe is, but he sho'll is black! I never seen nobody black as this. The black outside ain't even black as this. Never seen it, but Mama have. She say, when she was real little, when she was maybe even littler than me, Mama say she saw real black long time ago, so long, she said folk didn't even live inside. They lived outside, out in the night. She say sometime, when they stand out there, a star made them blacker. She said folk used to stand outside all day in a star they call *Sun* and just get blacker and blacker, and it didn't hurt and nobody even cared at all. Wayback when they didn't know it was dying.

"Come on, Nene."

That Mama. She poke her head in and stare at my face. She squinting like that dead star shining in her eye, like it too bright to see. I think I look the same, but I ain't sure. Maybe I'm not black enough? If it it's not black, ole joe black, the folk don't laugh. If I don't jump and bow, reel fast enough, the folk don't even smile. They just look and stare, look like the star in their eye, look like that old star shine so bright, the light fill the sky full of tears.

Djarkarta rising

no light
only the span of tongues
and this slow stirring of language
we reach across our history
to touch this science
choose words that conjure
an ancient burning name
   djarkarta
setting worlds into motion
words that splinter silence
drumming into bones

no room
for ashes and burnished urns
fashioned from sorrows ages old
we travel light
carry our dead in our heads
and move…

fleeing liquid cracks
in the ceiling
all debts paid
and paid again
the difference
is change
may time reveal
if it is better

while generations
drift through space
like shooting stars
       oh,
that brilliance there
that brilliance,
is it us,
rising?

The Grassdreaming Tree

That woman was always in shadow; no memory saved her from the dark. True, her star was not Sun but some other place. Nor did she come from this country call life. Maybe that's why she always lived with her shoulders turned back, walked with the caution of strangers—outside woman trying to sweep her way in. The grasshopper peddler, witchdoctor seller, didn't even have no name, no name. So folks didn't know where to place her. For all they know, she didn't even have no navel string, just them green humming things, look like dancing blades of grass. They look at her, with her no-name self, and they call her grasswoman.

Every morning she would pass through the black folks' land, carrying her enormous baskets. These she made herself, 'cause nobody else remembered. And they were made from grass so flimsy, they didn't even look like baskets, more like brown bubbles 'bout to pop. What they looked like were dying leaves dangling from her limbs, great curled wings that might flutter away, kicked up by a soft wind. Inside the baskets, the grasshoppers fluttered around and pranced, blue-green winged, long-legged things. The *click-clack, tap-tap* of the hoppers' limbs announced her arrival. A tattoo of drumbeats followed the grasswoman wherever she went, drumbeats so loud they rattled the windows and flung back shades:

Mama, the children cried, *Mama, look! Grasswoman comin'!*

And the hoppers would flood the streets. Their joy exchanged: the grasshoppers shouted and the children jumped, one heartbeat at a time. The woman would pull out her mouth harp and put the song to melody. The whole world was filled with their music.

But behind curtains drawn shut in frustration, the settlers suck-teethed dissatisfaction. They took the grasswoman's seeds and tried to crush them with suspicion, replacing the grasswoman's music with their own dark song—who did that white gal think she was? Where she come from and who in the world was her mama? Who told her she could come shuffling down their street, barefooted and grubby-toed, selling bugs and asking folk for food? The white ought to go on back to her proper place. *But the bugs are so sweet,* the children insisted. The parents shut their ears and stiffened their necks: No, no, and no again.

But the children didn't pay them no mind. The grasswoman's baskets were too full of songs to forget to play. One little girl, more hardheaded than most, disobeyed the edict and devoted herself to the enigmatic grasswoman. Her name was Mema, a big-eyed child with a head like a drum. She would wake early, plant her eyes on the cool window pane, waiting for the grasswoman to walk by. When the woman would come into view, Mema would rush down the stairs, *skip hop jump.* Bare feet running, she'd fly down the road and disappear among the swarm of grasshoppers spilling from the great leaf baskets. The Sun would sink, a red jack-ball sky, and still no word from Mema. Not a hide nor a hair they'd see, and at Mema's home, the folk would start pulling out their worries and polishing them up with spite.

Running barefoot, wild as that other.

Her daddy picked his switch and held it in his hand. Only her mama's soft words brought relief to the little girl's return. Hours later in the fullness of night, her daddy insisted on a reason, even if it was just the chalk line of truth:

Where she stay? Did you go to her house? Do she even have a house?

Her dwelling was an okro tree. She laid her head in the empty hollow of its great stone trunk. Mema told them the tree was sacred, that God had planted its roots upside down so they touched sky.

Daddy turned to his wife, pointing the blame finger at her. *See, the white's been filling her head. That* tree *ain't got no roots. Whole world made of stone, thick as your head. Couldn't grow a tree to save your life.*

The girl spoke up, hoppers hidden all in her hair. *It's true, Mama, it's true. The tree got a heart and sometime it get real sad. The old woman say the okro tree can kill itself, say it can do it by fire. Even if nobody strike a match.*

Mama just shook her head. Daddy roll his eyes. *Stone tree dead by fire?*

Child say, *It's true.*

What foolishness, the mama say, and she draw her daughter close to her, tucking her big head under her chin, far and away from her daddy's reach. Then the man left, taking his anger with him, and he handed it over to the other settlers. At the lodge they all agreed: the grasswoman's visits had to end. They couldn't kill her—to do so would offend the land and the children and the women, so whatever was done, they agreed to give the deed some thought.

Next day, the grasshopper seller returned. The drumbeats-of-joy wings and legs swept through the air. Even the settlers stopped to listen. Spite was in their mouths, but the rhythm took hold of their feet. After all, that white was bringing with her such beauty none had ever seen. None could resist her grasshoppers' winged anthem, nor their blue-greened glory, shining and iridescent as God's first land. The sight was like nothing else in this new and natural world. They'd left their stories in that other place, and now the grasshopper peddler was selling them back.

The folk began to wonder: where in the name of all magic did she get such miraculous creatures? Couldn't have been from this land where the soil was pink and ruddy and no grass grew anywhere save for under glass-topped houses carefully tended by the science ones. They had packed up all their knowledge and carried it with them in small black stones that were not opened until they'd settled on this other shore with its two bright stars folk just looked at and called Sun 'cause some habits just hard to break.

And where indeed? Whoever heard tale of grasshoppers where they ain't no grass? Where, if they had already brought the most distant of their new land to heel?

The grasshopper peddler only answered with a chuckle, her two cheeks puffed out like she 'bout to whistle. But she don't speak, just smiling so, skin all red and blistered, folk wonder how she could stand one Sun, let alone two. They began to weigh their own suspicions, take them apart and spread them in their hand: could it be that white gal had a right to enter a world that was closed to them? And how she remember, old as she is, if they forget? But then they set about cutting her down: the woman lived in trees, nothing but grasshoppers as company, got to be crazy, laying up there with all them bugs. And where they come from anyway?

Whether it was 'cause folk couldn't stand her or folk was puzzled and secretly admired her strangeful ways, the grasswoman became the topic of talk scattered all over the town. Her presence began to fill the length of conversations, unexpected empty moments, great and small. The more people bought from her, dipping their hands in the great leaf baskets, the more their homes became filled with the sweet songs of wings, songs that made them think of summers and tall grass up to your knees, and bushes that reach out to smack your thighs when you walk by, and trees that lean over to brush the top of your hand, soft like a granddaddy's touch—land that whispered secrets and filled the air with the seeds of green growing things.

Such music fell strangely on the settlers' ears that bent only to hear the quickstep march of progress. In a land of pink soil as hard as earth diamonds, it was clear that they held little in common with their new home. And could it be that the grasswoman's hoppers were nibbling at the settlers' sense of self, turning them into aliens in this far land they'd claimed as their own? Or was it that white gal at fault, that nonworking hussy who insisted on being, insisting on breathing when most of her seed was extinct, existing completely outside their control, a wild weed of a thing, and unaware of the duties of her race? The traitors who traded her singing grasshoppers for bits of crust and crumbs of food hidden in pockets, handed out with a sidelong glance, should have known that after all that had been given, as far as they had traveled, leaving the dying ground of one world, to let the dead bury their dead, there was no room for the old woman's bare-toed feet on their stone streets.

The head folk were annoyed at such disobedience, concerned at the blatant disrespect for order and decorum, blaming it on the times and folks giving in to the children's soft ways, children too young to remember the hardness of skin, how it could be used like a thick-walled prison to deny the blood within. Too young to remember how the sun looked like wet stars in morning dew, and how it walked on wide feet and stood on the sky's shoulders, spreading its light all over that other place. How it warmed them and baked them like fresh bread, until their brown skins shone with the heart of it.

But the grasswoman was overstepping her bounds, repeating that same dance, treading on sacred ground that she did not belong to. Not enough that her folk had stolen the other lands and sucked them dry with their dreaming, not enough that they had taken the names and knowledge and twisted them so that nobody could recall their meaning, bad enough that every tale had to be retold by them to be heard true, that no sight was seen unless their eyes had seen it, no new ground covered unless they were there to stake it, no old herb could heal without them finding new ways to poison it. Now she had stolen their stories, the song-bits of self, and had trained grasshoppers, like side-show freaks, to drum back all the memories they had tried to forget.

Even the children, thanks to her gifting, were beginning to forget themselves. They hummed strange tunes that they could not have remembered, told new lies that sounded like cradle tales of old, stories 'bout spiders they called uncle in a language nobody knowed, and hopped around like brown crickets, mimicking dances long out of step. They were becoming more like children of the dust than of the pink stone of their birth, with its twin Sun and an anvil for sky.

And a small loss it was. They had traded the soft part of themselves, their stories and songs, the fingerprints of a culture, for that deemed useful. Out went the artifacts that had once defined a people. Only once did they yearn for the past, when creatures could be swept away depending on their appearance. The grasswoman had even took hold of their dreams. The parents were determined to stop this useless dreaming. They knew if they were to live again, to plant new seed, they had to abandon all thoughts of their past existence. What they wanted were new habits, new languages, new stories to mine in this strange borderland in the backbone of sky. So the command was clear: the stone streets were off limits. You couldn't go out anymore. Curtains were drawn, and the houses shut their great eyelids.

⤙

Order seemed to rule again, but it didn't last long. That's when things began to happen. Doors covered with strange carvings and cupboards filled with stones. Furniture was arranged in circles and drawers mismatched and swapped round.

At the Kings' house:

Who been in this cupboard?

No one, none had. Grandmama King got mad; everybody in the house knew that her teeth were kept there. Now the little glass dish was full of stones, and from every shelf the stones grinned back at her like pink gums.

At the Greenes' house:

Who scattered grasshopper wings 'cross my desk?

No one, nobody, not anyone, none was the reply. Daddy Greene choked back disgust. *"Grasshoppers all in my cup,"* he muttered, *"Damn crickets."*

At the head folks' offices:

"Who let them bugs in?"

Nobody had. The bugs had filled the bottoms of file drawers and hid in official-looking papers, fresh piles of pellets and grasshopper dung on settler documents stamped with official seals, the droppings among the deeds for land with their names scrawled across them like spider webs.

On the tail of all this, a general uproar gripped the settlement. The settlers held a straighten-it-out meeting, hoping to make a decision. They'd held off on the grasswoman's fate for too long, and now it was time to come to the end of it. They assembled at the home of Mema's daddy. The girl slipped out of her bed and stood at the door, listening to the groans and threats. She didn't even wait for their answer. She rushed off down the stone streets and slipped through a crack in the glass, in the direction of the grasswoman's stone tree. There, she found the old woman settling herself by the okro's belly, a dark stone cavern that swallowed the light. Her great leaf basket rested in her lap. Another one at her side toppled over, empty.

"They gon' get you," the child say.

Mema was gasping for breath. The air was much thinner outside the settlement's glass dome. But the grasswoman didn't act put out. She seemed to know and had gathered her two great baskets and released the blue-green winged things. But Mema could not see where they had gone, and she wondered how they would survive without the grasswoman tending them.

The little girl tried harder. She scratched her drumskull and tilted her head, staring into the old woman's face with a question. Never before had the grasswoman meant so much.

"Run away," the child cried. *"You still got time."*

But the grasshopper peddler just set herself at ease, didn't look like she could be bothered. Her hair and skin looked gray and hard, like the stringy meat on a bone. She pushed the baskets aside, pressed her palms into the ground, and rose with some effort. She stood, sucking a stone, patting her dirt skirt, and smoothing the faded rags with gentle strokes. Her hair hung 'bout her eyes in a matted tangle. She seemed to be looking at the horizon. Soon the Sun would set and only a few night stars would remain peering through a veil of clouds.

"*Go on, child,*" the grasswoman said. "*Fire coming soon.*"

Mema hung back afraid. She glanced at the grasswoman, at her tattered clothes that smelled like the earth Mema had never known, at her knotted hair that looked like it could eat any comb, and her sad eyes that looked like that old word, *sea.* If only the grasswoman could be like that, still but moving, far and away from here.

"*Why don't you run? They gon' hurt you if they catch you,*" Mema said.

The old woman stood outside the hollow of the tree, motionless, as if time had carried her off. She stared at the child and held out her withered hand. Mema reached for it, slid her fingers into the grasswoman's cool, dry palm.

"*Mema, there is more to stone than what we see. Sometime stone carry water, and sometime it carry blood.* Bloodfire. *Remember the story I told you?*" Mema nodded. The grasswoman squeezed her hand and placed it on the trunk of the stone tree. "*In this place you must know just how and when to tap it. Only the pure will know.*"

The girl bowed her head, blinked back tears. The tree felt cold to her touch, a tall silent stone, the color of night.

Now you must go, the grasswoman said. She released Mema's hand and smiled. A tiny grasshopper with bold black and red stripes appeared in the space of her cool touch. Its tiny antennas tapped into her palm as if to taste it. Mema held the hopper in her cupped palm and watched the old woman, standing in her soiled clothing among the black branches of the tree. To the child, the grasswoman's face seemed to waver, like a trick in the fading light. Her skin was the wax of berries, her tangled hair as innocent as vine leaves.

Mema pressed her toes against the stone ground, reluctant to go. She looked up at the huge tree that was not a tree, as if asking it for protection, its trunk more mountain than wood, its roots stabbing at the sky, the base rising from what might have been rich soil long ago.

Can you hear the heart? asked the old woman.

The child recalled the grasswoman's tale. The heart-stone was where the tree's spirit slept, in the polished stone the color of blood, the strength of fire. Whoever harmed the okro tree would bear its mark for the rest of their life. Mema stood there, her face screwed up, shoulders slumped, as if she already carried the okro's stone burden. With gentle wings, the grasshopper pulsed in her cupped hands.

❧

The settlers began their noisy descent. They surrounded the stone clearing, outside their city of glass. The little girl fled, her heart in her drum, hid, and watched from the safety of a fledgling stone tree. She saw the grasswoman rise and greet the folk with open palms, an ancient sign of peace. The curses started quick, then the shouts and the kicks, then finally, a stone shower. Tiny bits of rock, pieces scraped up in anger from the sky's stone floor were flung up, a sudden hailstorm. The old woman didn't even appear to be startled, and her straight back, once curved with age and humility, showed no fear. The stones came, and the blood flowed, tiny drops of it warming the ground, staining the black stone. They crushed her baskets with their heels and bound her wrists, pushed her up the long dark road. A group of settlers followed close behind, muttering, leaving the child alone in the night. The girl hesitated, her drumskull tilted back with thought, her neck full of tears. After a long silence, she stepped forward, facing the empty stone tree. Then it happened: the heartstone of the okro crumbled, black shards of stone shattered like star dust. She stepped gingerly among the colored shards. The dark crystals turned to red powder under her feet, stone blood strewn all over the ground. With a cup-winged rhythm, the hopper pulsed angrily in her shaking hand.

Suddenly, the child made up her mind. She dashed off through the stone clearing the children now called wood, crushing blood-red shards beneath her feet. The hopper safely tucked in her clasped hand, she noiselessly scurried behind the restless, shuffling mob of stonethrowers. Her ears picked up the thread of their whispers. They were taking the grasswoman to a jail that had not been built. *The well,* someone had cried, a likely prison as any. Mema shuddered to think of her friend all alone down there. Would she be afraid in the cold abandoned hole that held no water? Would she be hungry? And then it struck her: she had never seen the grasswoman eat. Like the hoppers, she sucked on stone, holding it in her mouth as if it were a bit of sweet hard candy. What did she do with the food they had given her, the table scraps and treats stolen and bartered for stories woven from a dead-dying world?

The grasshopper thumped against the hollow of her palm as if to answer. Mema stroked the tiny wings to calm its anxious drumbeat. Maybe the hoppers ate the crumbs, the child thought as she crouched in the blackness beside the old woman's walled prison. The well had gone dry in the days of the first settlers, and now that massive pumping stations had been built, the folk no longer needed stone holes to tap the world's subterranean caverns. Hidden in darkness, the grasshopper trembling in her palm, Mema began to suffocate with fear. The grasswoman had taught her how to sing without words, without air or drum. Was there any use of dancing anymore, if the grasswoman could not share the music? If the world around her had been stripped of its beauty, its story magic? And in the sky was silence, just as in the stone tree, no heartstone beat its own ancient rhythm anymore.

The grasswoman's voice reached her from within the well, drifting over its chipped black stone covered with dust. Now Mema could see the soft edges of her friend's shape, her body pressed in a corner of darkness. If she peered closely, letting her eyes adjust to the shadow and the light, she could just barely make out the contours of the old woman's forehead, the brightness of her eyes as they blinked in the night. Voices made night, is what she heard, felt more than saw—the motion of the old woman's great eyelids blinking as she called to her. The grasswoman's voice sounded like a tongue coated in blood, pain rooted in courage, the resignation of old age. Mema drew back, afraid. What if someone saw her there, perched on the side of the well, whispering to the unhappy prisoner in the belly of night? Footsteps called out, as if in answer.

Quickly, the child jumped off the wall and fell, bruising a knee as she crawl-walked over to hide behind a row of trash cans. One lone guard came swinging his arms and shaking his head. He leaned an elbow on the lip and craned his neck to peer into the well.

May I? the grasswoman asked, and she put her stone harp to her lips and tried to blow. But the notes sounded strained, choked out of her bruised throat and sore lips, where the settlers had smacked and cuffed her. The guard snorted, became suspicious. *Throw it up,* he ordered, and the harp was hurled up and over the well's mouth with the last of the old woman's strength. The guard tried to catch it, but it crashed on the ground. The dissonant sound made Mema gasp and cup her ears. *There'll be no more music from you, 'til you tell us where you come from,* the guard said, but in his heart, he didn't really didn't want to know. Truth was, none of them did. They feared her, the grasswoman who came like a flower, some wretched wild weed they'd thought they'd stamped out in that other desert and fled like a shadow, disappearing into their most secret thoughts. The well was silent. The guard glanced at the little broken mouth harp scattered on the street. They'd probably want him to get it, as evidence, something else they could cast against the old woman, but he wasn't going to touch it. No telling where the harp had been, and he certainly didn't want nothing to do with nothing that had been sitting up in her mouth. So he turned on his heel and headed for the dim lights down the street, leaving the grasswoman quiet behind him.

No, not quiet. Crying? A soft sound, like a child awakened from sleep. He shook his head in pity. He didn't know what other secrets the folk expected to drag out of their prisoner. She was just an old woman, no matter her skin, and anyway, what could they prove against the street peddler, guilty of nothing but being where being was no longer a sin.

When the guard's last echo disappeared into the night, Mema crept back to the well and picked up the stone harp's broken pieces. She held the instrument in her free hand and released the grasshopper on the well's edge. She half-expected it to fly away, but he sat there, flexing his legs in a slow rhythmic motion, preening. She clasped the harp together again, sat down on her haunches, and began to blow softly. As the child curled up in the warmth of her own roundness, she set off to sleep, drifting in a strange lullaby. She could vaguely hear the grasshopper accompanying her, a mournful ticking, and the grasswoman softly crying below, the sound like grieving. *Maybe*, she thought as her lids slowly closed, *maybe the grasswoman could hear it, too, and would be comforted.*

She awoke in a kingdom of drumming, the ground thumping beneath her head and her feet. The hoppers! A thousand of them covered the bare ground all around her and filled the whole street. Squatting and jumping, the air was jubilant, but the child could not imagine the cause of celebration. *The grasswoman is free!* she thought and tried to rise, but the grasshoppers covered every inch of her, as if she too were part of the glass city's stone streets. All around they stared at her, slantfaced and bandwinged, spurthroated and bowlegged. It was still night—the twin Sun had long receded from the sky, and even the lamps of the city were fast asleep. Nothing could explain the hoppers' arousal, their joy, or their number, or why they had not retreated in the canopy of night. Not even the world, in all its universal dimensions, seemed a big enough field for them to wing through.

Mema carefully rose, brushing off handfuls of the hoppers, careful not to crush their wings. The air hummed with the sound of a thousand drums, each hopper signaling its own rapid-fire rhythm. They seemed to preen and stir, turnaround, as if letting the stars warm their wings and their belly. The child tried to mind each step, but it was difficult in the dark, and finally she gave up and leaned into the well's gaping mouth. *Grasswoman?* she called, and stepped back in surprise. The drumming sound was coming from deep within the well. She placed her hands above the well's lip and felt a fresh wave of wings and legs pouring from it, the iridescent wings sparkling and flowing like water. The grasswoman had vanished; the place had lost all memory of her, it seemed. Mema called the old woman, but received no answer, only the drumming and the flash of wings.

She decided to return to the okro, the stone tree where for a time, the grasswoman had lived. There was no longer any other place she might go. Some pitied the grasswoman, but none enough to take her in—no street, nor house; only the stone tree's belly. As Mema walked along, the hoppers seemed to follow her, and after a time, her movements stopped being steps and felt like wind. It was as if the hoppers carried her along with them, and not the other way around. They were leading the child to the okro, to the stone forest, back to the place where the story begin.

Mema arrived at the grasswoman's door and looked at the stone floor covered with blood-red shards, the heartstone ground into powder. The okro was no longer dull stone, but was covered in a curious pattern, black with finely carved red lines, pulsing like veins. She stood at the door of the great trunk and entered, head bowed, putting distance between herself and time. Was there any use in waiting for the old woman? Mema blinked back tears, listened for the hoppers' drum. Surely by now, the grasswoman had vanished, taking her stories and her strange ways with her, a fugitive of the blackfolk's world again. The child took the stone harp and placed it to her mouth. She lulled herself in its shattered rhythm, listening with an ear outside the world, a place that confused her, listening as the hoppers kept time with their hindlegs and tapping feet. She played and dreamed, dreamed and played, but if she had listened harder, she would have heard the arrival of a different beat.

There she is! That old white heffa inside the tree!

Spiteful steps surrounded the okro, crushing the hoppers underfoot.

It's the woman with her mouth harp. Go on play, then. We'll see how well you dance!

They tossed their night torches aside, raised their mallets, and flung their pickaxes through the air. The hammers crushed the ancient stone, metal teeth bit at stone bark. Inside, the girl child had unleashed a dream: her hair was turning into tiny leaves, her legs into lean timber. Her fingers dug rootlike into the stone soil. The child was in another realm, she was flesh turning into wood, wood into stone, girl child as tree, stone tree of life. Red hot blades of grass burst in tight bubbles at her feet, pulsing from the okro's stone floor, a crimson wave of lava roots erupting into mythic drumbeats and bursting wingsongs. Somewhere she heard a ring shout chorus, hot cry of the settlers' voices made night, the ground fluttering all around them, the hoppers surrounding the bubbling tree, ticking, wing-striking, leg-raising, romp-shaking vibrations splitting the stone floor, warming in the groundswell of heat. And from the grassdreaming tree, blood-red veins writhing, there rose the grasswoman's hands. They stroked crimson flowers that blossomed into rubies and fell on the great stone floor. Corollas curled, monstrous branches born and released, petal-like on the crest of black flames. The child's drumskull throbbed as she concentrated, straining to hear the grasswoman's call, to remember her lessons, how to make music without words, without air and drum, and her thoughts floated in the air, red hot embers of brimstone blues drifting toward the glass-walled city.

And as the ground erupted beneath them, the settlers stood in horror, began to run and flee, but the children, the children rose from tucked-in beds, the tiny backs of their hands erasing sleep, their soft feet ignoring slippers and socks, toes running barefoot over the stone streets and the rocks, they came dancing, *skip hop jump,* through the glass door into the stone wood, waves of hoppers at their heels, their blue-green backs arched close to the ground as they hopped from stone to hot stone, drumming as they went, bending like strong reeds, like green grass lifting toward the night. And that was when Mema felt the sting of blaze, when the voices joined her in the song of ash, and the stone's new heart beat an ancient rhythm, the children singing, the hoppers drumming, the settlers crying.

And when the Sun rose, the land one great shadow of fire and ash, the hoppers lay in piles at their feet. They had shed their skins that now looked like finger-prints, the dust of the children blowing in the wind all around them. And that night, when the twin Sun set, the settlers would think of their lost children and remember the old woman who ate stones and cried grasshoppers for tears.

Biography

Sheree Renée Thomas is a native of Memphis. A Cave Canem Fellow and a New York Foundation of the Arts Fellow, her short stories, poetry, and articles have appeared in various publications, including *storySouth, Callaloo, Colorlines, Essence Magazine, Upscale, VIBE, Obsidian III, Harpur Palate, The Washington Post Book World, Meridians, African Voices, Drumvoices Revue, Black Renaissance/Renaissance Noire as* well as in several anthologies, including *Mojo: Conjure Stories, Hurricane Blues, Role Call, Bum Rush the Page: A Def Poetry Jam, The Ringing Ear, MYTHIC 2, Southern Revival, Bronx Biannual,* and *So Long Been Dreaming: Postcolonial Science Fiction and Fantasy.* A mother of two daughters and a teaching artist, Sheree is the editor of two anthologies (*Dark Matter: A Century of Speculative Fiction from the African Diaspora* and *Dark Matter: Reading the Bones,* winner of the 2001 and 2005 World Fantasy Award). *Shotgun Lullabies* is the first collection of her work.